BRUTAL BEAST

PLANET OF KINGS BOOK 4

LEE SAVINO &

TABITHA BLACK

SILVERWOOD PRESS

Only an Omega can save the Beast...
Once, I was a golden prince, full of promise. Then the curse
came for my parents. I did everything I could to save them.
I failed.
Now, I am a monster, scarred and dangerous. I remain in
the shadows, ruling my kingdom from afar, feared by
everyone I fight to protect.
My subjects stay away from me and my haunted castle. But
one stubborn woman refused to heed the warnings: an
Omega named Rose.
She came to demand my help.
I'll never let her go.

CONTENT WARNINGS:

The Planet of Kings books are dark omegaverse tales with
adult themes. Read at your own risk.
Please follow this link for a full list of content warnings for
each individual title:
www.leesavino.com/brutal-series-tropes-and-content-
warnings/

DEDICATION

For Judy.
We can't thank you enough.

ONE

Bestian

I DREAM OF AN OMEGA. SHE IS TINY COMPARED TO ME, as Omegas are. She's fragile and elegant, with dark skin and eyes, her hair, a soft brown halo around her head. Hidden fire gleams in the tight curls—there are bright jewels set at her ears and threaded through her hair. Her perfume twines around me, pulling me closer, awakening my Alpha need. It's been years since I last scented an Omega. There are none left in my kingdom.

Except for her. My queen. I draw her into my arms. It's the work of a moment to nudge her thighs apart and sink into her. She shudders, opening to me slowly, accepting my cock.

For the first time ever, I'm balls-deep in an Omega, relishing her perfect moonflower scent. Her perfume brings my dominance to the fore. My muscles strain as I thrust deep. She moans, spreads her legs wider, and takes it all. Her slick gushes between us, its heady scent intoxicating me even more.

My knot swells. Soon, I will fill her with my seed to the

point where it will overflow around my cock. My canines sharpen to dagger points in my mouth. It's time to mark my precious Omega. She will belong to me, our souls bonded forever. My power will be hers, and she will always be mine. She arches her neck for my bite, ready for me to claim her, and that's when I see it: The Red Death.

The rash rolls up her skin, scarlet blisters ravaging her beauty, like red fire crackling up a lush hillside, leaving ash and destruction in its wake. Her lips crack and her eyes grow hollow. She's dying right in front of me, succumbing to the same curse that took my parents.

And I am impotent to stop it.

My roar rings out, shaking my ruined castle on its foundations. Dust rains down from the rafters. How long was I asleep? When was the last time I had the *whisps*, my magical wind servants, clean in here?

It's time, something whispers inside of me. *Make ready.*

I scrub my face, my fingers tracing the harsh ridges of my scarred skin. Once, I was handsome. Once, I was beloved by my kingdom and parents alike. When I was much younger, I had hope for my future, for finding a mate. My perfect Omega, the one I was born to claim.

Now I have nothing. There are no Omegas left on Ulfaria. And if the curse has come again...

I cannot stop it. I have no hope, only an empty castle and a ravaged face, and the memory of a dream.

Rose

I'm startled awake with a roar echoing in my ears. I peer through the gloom but see nothing. The only sounds are the creaking of the trees outside my window and the tentative trills of the lizard-like creatures that sit on the branches and sing like birds.

It must have been my dream. I dreamt I was in a ruined castle filled with vines and flowers blooming in the darkness all around. A breeze tugged at my skirts, pulling me forward towards... something? Someone? A great shape in the center of a dusty ballroom. A statue—or a figure standing so still, he might as well have been one. He was humanoid, but huge. On Earth, he'd be a giant. Here on Ulfaria, he'd be an Alpha, bigger than any other I've seen.

My skin tingles with the memory and I rub my face. It was just a dream.

A cool wind blows over my bed, ruffling the quilt. Somehow, in the night, my window cracked open. I jump up to close it but it catches on a vine. Overnight, a silvery-green tendril grew up the side of Ma's cottage and snaked inside.

That's some fast growing weed. I like plants—back home, they'd say I have a green thumb—but Ulfarri flora takes some getting used to.

I push the vine out and shut the window. It looks like more creeping plants grew over this side of the cottage. I'll make time to trim them back later today. Ma will know why it grows so fast.

Just another weird alien plant on this weird alien planet. Same old, same old.

I unwrap my hair and shake out my braids, then dress in my blouse and loose skirts. Everything is boho peasant chic around here. At least I have good sturdy boots. I wait to put those on until I've slipped out of my room and tiptoed down the hall past Ma's bedroom. Her door is shut. Usually she's awake earlier than I am. I lift my skirts, easing down the creaky stairs. Ma wasn't feeling well last night. I want to let her sleep.

Ma's cottage is small by Ulfarri standards, barely more than a hut. But to me it's nice and roomy, especially after my cramped NYC apartment. Everything is supersized on this planet. Ma—the Ulfarri who took me in—is considered small, and she's taller than I am. And I'm five ten. I worked as a model back home.

I set about packing up the vials and herbal packets we've spent all week making. Ma's potions are considered medicine around here. There's enough to fill two baskets, which will be awkward to carry, but I can deal. I can handle one morning at the market and let Ma sleep in. It's the least I can do, after all she's done for me.

I owe her so much more.

The front door of the cottage sticks when I try to open it. I set down the baskets and throw all my weight against it to force it open.

Thick, black vines have grown all over the stoop. They weren't here yesterday. They must have sprouted up overnight. I prod them with my boot. First the tendril at my window, now these.

I kick a few out of the way until I can open the door further, and scrape the rest of them off. I'm as quiet as I can be, but a wheezing cough echoes down the stairs.

"Rose?" Ma calls from her bedroom. Her scratchy voice makes me wince.

So much for sneaking out. I move back toward the stairs and call up to her. "Sorry about the racket, Ma." She's not my mother but when she took me in, her full name—Matron Marphel—somehow got shortened to *Ma* in my head. "Go back to sleep."

"You're going to market?"

"I told you I would. Since you weren't feeling well last night, I had hoped you'd sleep in this morning. I'll be back soon."

"Very well." She sounds so weak, I hesitate, suddenly worried about leaving her.

"Are you sure you don't want me to make you some tea before I go?" I turn too quickly and knock a bundle of dry *dola* leaves to the floor. I hang the fallen bundle back up beside the others. We harvested the *dola* last week, and they fill the cottage with their rich herbal scent, a cross between sage and oregano.

"No, child. I'm sure I'll be up in no time. I can make my own tea."

"You're supposed to be resting."

"I'll be fine. Don't forget your cloak."

"I won't." Going over to the rack, I stick my tongue out at my heavy cloak and grab it off the hook. It was too much to hope Ma would forget, and I could leave it behind. The morning air is cool and still, but once the suns rise, it will be hot, and I'll be stuck sweating with my hood up.

"Remember, if you see any Alphas—"

"If I see any Alphas, I'll keep my head down. I won't look them in the eye. I won't talk to them," I promise. Alphas never buy anything from our booth anyway.

"And did you take your medicine?"

"Of course," I say before remembering that I forgot this morning. Oh well. I took it yesterday. And I'll take it before I get back. Taking a dose a few hours late won't hurt.

"Good." Ma's weak voice sounds relieved. Guilt stabs me. She's pathological about the weird potion she makes me drink every day. And about avoiding Alphas. "Remember, don't speak to the soldiers," she repeats. "Stay away from them."

Well, I was planning on slapping one on the ass, but now that you've reminded me twice, I won't. I bite back my sarcasm. Ma is the closest thing I have to family on this alien planet and I stuff my New York City girl rudeness down for her.

Besides, people here don't get sarcasm. Which is just fantastic. Sarcasm is my superpower.

On a whim, before heading back to the door, I grab a large, sheathed kitchen knife and fasten it to my belt. If Ma is so worried about Alphas, maybe I should be armed. Too bad she doesn't have some alien form of Mace.

With a basket handle slung over each shoulder, I head off down the little pathway which will take me to the main road to the market, Ma's warnings still ringing in my ears.

The suns are rising in the sky—yes, suns, plural—and it's shaping up to be a hot day. A breeze darts and tugs at my skirts. It feels good, but as I get closer to the village, I pull my hood up over my braids.

At this rate, by the time I'm done at the market, I'll be tempted to strip everything off and dunk myself in the nearby river. I've done it before, but only at night. Ma frowns on my skinny-dipping ventures. "It's not safe," she scolds. "There might be Alpha patrols nearby."

She's pathological about Alphas. But Ma knows best.

A few months ago, I woke up on a riverbank with absolutely no clue where I was—or even really *who* I was. I know my name, my age, and occasionally I'll have flashes of random memories, but otherwise, zilch. Even my memories don't feel like mine. Sometimes, when looking at my reflection in the river or water basin, I'll flash back to looking in a mirror while a makeup artist painted eyeshadow in brilliant peacock shades onto my face for a fashion show. I'll recall strutting down the catwalk wearing outrageous designs, but the impressions are faded. Like clips of a stranger's home movie, glimpses of another life.

Ma was out gathering herbs when she found me. I was dressed in a flimsy nightshirt, dazed, scared out of my mind, and thirstier than I ever remember being. When I first saw her—a ridiculously tall, older-looking woman with papery mauve skin covered in royal blue markings, and dressed in a cloak—I thought I was hallucinating. But she was so kind. She gave me something cool and sweet to drink, wrapped me in her cloak, and took me back to her hut.

And that's how I learned I was in the kingdom of Medela, on the planet Ulfaria. A different freaking *planet*! We don't know how I got here, or why. According to Ma, I'm lucky she found me, and not a troop of Alphas.

She's never told me why she's so paranoid about Alphas and my being near them. Most of the Alphas around these parts are soldier types on patrol, and I haven't felt threatened by them. Sure, they're huge, and they tend to grunt more than they talk, but other than that...

Society here on Ulfaria is basically divided into three main groups—Alphas, Betas, and Omegas. Alphas are bigger, stronger, and fertile as fuck, according to Ma (although she put it differently). They're almost always male, and dominant, and used to getting what they want. All the kings of this planet are Alphas, and so are all of the soldiers and warriors. Betas make up the majority of the population, although I'm not sure if things always were that way, or if that's just the case now because Omegas are rare to non-existent. In any case, Betas can do pretty much anything—aside from become king—but they can't provide Alphas with offspring. Only Omegas can do that. Ma says Omegas are fertile as fuck, too—although again, she uses different language.

And then there's me. A human. A stranger in a strange land.

Ahead on the path, a group of soldiers is standing guard. I have to walk past them to get into the village. I can tell they're Alphas because they're a head taller than everyone else—which is already a foot taller than I am.

I pull my hood tighter to hide my face, and fix my eyes on the ground. It's time to get to work. The sooner I sell our goods, the sooner I can get back home to Ma.

TWO

Rose

IT DOESN'T TAKE ME LONG TO SELL OUT OF MA'S herbal potions and powders. The villagers know our stall, and many have standing orders they pick up regularly. Today, most of them approach slowly, looking around for Ma, but lose their wariness when I tell them she's only resting. They grab their purchases and leave, not hanging around for small talk.

All around the market, giant Alphas stand guard. I've never seen so many before. Normally they're easy to avoid, but today they're everywhere. Good thing Ma isn't here, or she'd make me hide under the counter.

I need to get her to tell me why Alphas have her so freaked out. I haven't probed because I get the impression there's some trauma there. They're bigger and badder than everyone else, and everyone treads lightly around them, not just Ma.

A trio of merchants sweeps past my booth. One of them is waving his hands, his tone heated. "And now the king expects a tithe. In his father's day—"

The speaker's buddy nudges him, calling his attention to the knot of guards standing by the fountain. The guards glower at him and he drops his hands, swallowing his outrage. As one, the Beta merchants turn and duck into the nearest tavern.

That's why people seem tense today. It's their equivalent of tax season.

A customer raps on the side of my booth to get my attention. "Do you have any *jahro* root?" His voice is raspy.

"No." I don't need to check my empty baskets. "I'm out of everything." I love what Ma is teaching me about herbs and tinctures, but today, the marketplace vibe is weird. It's time to count my coins and move on.

The customer leans in and grabs my arm. "Please, I need medicine. The curse has come again—"

I shrink away, freeing my arm, leaving the man clutching at air. The Ulfarri is in my face and his hood has fallen back to reveal yellow skin flushed scarlet on his cheeks and neck.

A shadow slides over us. An Alpha guard pushes close, towering over the smaller Ulfarri. He grunts something, and the Beta cringes and shuffles away.

If I had any *jahro* root left, I would have given it to the Beta. I didn't want him grabbing at me, but the guard's behavior was harsh.

Now I have to deal with the giant Alpha. If Ma hears about this, she will shit a brick.

He towers over me, his impressive muscles glistening in the sunlight. His skin is pale green, and his hair, beard, and markings are all various shades of blue.

Even though I should be used to it by now, I still can't get over the way Ulfarri people have such a wide range of skin and hair color combinations. I have yet to see anyone with typical human skin tones—from any region on Earth—

but Ma says there are Ulfarri with dark hair and skin like mine, far up the coast. Ulfarri also have full-body, tattoo-esque markings, which I obviously lack. I can blend in, as long as I wear my cloak so people don't look too closely. One more reason to wear a hood.

The Alpha turns his head and meets my gaze. His eyes narrow and I take a step back.

My hood has slipped off. A prickle of panic tickles my spine. I bend, pretending to fuss with the pouch at my waist, where I've hidden the silver coins I've earned today. The knife is tucked into my belt beside it, still in its sheath. I let my fingers play over it for a moment. With my head still bowed, I slide the hood back up, praying the soldier will stop paying attention to me.

The Alpha grunts something I don't catch. I dip my head in answer and hope that's the right response. It must be, because after a few endless seconds, he moves on.

I grab my baskets. Time to skedaddle.

It's sweltering hot, especially in this cloak. Sweat trickles down my back, making my dress itch. Too bad I can't jump in the river—I'm burning up in this midday heat. I should head straight home, but my stomach won't let me pass by my favorite booth that sells sweet cakes. I stop to buy some for lunch. Leelah, the one who bakes them, is distracted, constantly peering around and beyond me as she puts together my order.

"What's going on?" I ask.

"Tensions are high," she says in a whisper, tucking a strand of bright orange hair behind her pointed bronze ear. "They always get like this when it's time to pay the king's tithe. Not to mention, there's some kind of sickness going around. My father says he hasn't seen symptoms like it since —" She falls silent, lowering her head and busying herself with wrapping my cakes. A shadow falls over the stall.

It's the Alpha from before. Did he follow me? *Shitshitshit—*

"Here you go," Leelah chirps, handing me my package. She turns her smile to the soldier. "What can I get for you?"

He mumbles something that sounds more like a growl than words, but she obviously understands him just fine, since she nods and starts putting items together.

When I first arrived, I was able to understand Ma even though there was no way she was speaking English. After looking me over carefully, she deduced I had been given some kind of translation chip. I can feel the bump behind my ear, but I don't like to touch it so I avoid it as much as I can. It took me a while but now I'm used to it translating speech in my head, although I don't think I'll ever stop struggling when I hear the Alphas talk.

The soldier and I are both watching Leelah fill his order. I should leave but I haven't paid yet, and I want to know what else Leelah has heard about this mystery illness. Knowledge is power, after all, and if Ma *does* have it...

The hair on my arms lifts. The Alpha is staring at me. His eyes are slightly unfocused, and his nostrils flare as he inhales slowly. Is he... *smelling* me?

I take a step sideways, away from him, and surreptitiously duck my head to sniff my cloak. Did I sweat off my deodorant? Ma makes this herbal balm that works wonders, but maybe it's worn off.

"Here you go." Leelah comes to the rescue, holding the bag out for the soldier.

He blinks, then turns his head back to face her. "Thanks," he mutters, taking his order from her.

"No charge," Leelah says, her voice tight. "Thank you for your service to the king."

The Alpha grunts his assent, and leaves.

My shoulders droop and I let my breath ease out of me.

Being the object of that stare was intense. If Ma ever finds out I drew the attention of a big bad Alpha—twice—she'll never let me come to the market again.

"Are you all right?" There's a little crease of concern on Leelah's brow.

"Of course. But Matron started feeling sick last night. Should I be worried?"

"Was she flushed?"

I hesitate, trying to remember how she looked the last time I saw her. "Maybe a little?"

"Oh, no." The furrow in Leelah's brow deepens before she mutters under her breath, "The Red Death."

My heart drops straight through my stomach into my boots. "That doesn't sound good," I manage.

"It hasn't been confirmed yet but there are whispers that this is another curse just like the Red Death. Of course, it might not be—"

"A curse? What sort of curse?"

"It starts with a rash. The skin turns a deep crimson. Then a wheezing cough. A fever. Then..." She bites her lip. "It gets worse. The whole body gradually hardens—like it's turning to stone."

Oh fuck, this is not good at all. As much as I want to run away, I need to hear all of this. I have to be able to help Ma if this is what she has.

"Victims of it feel like they're burning, like they can't breathe, and sleep is impossible due to the pain. Death is slow... but inevitable."

"How slow?" I croak. I feel dizzy.

She shrugs. "Depends on how healthy the person was to start with. Days... weeks... when it last swept the kingdom, sometimes people were able to hang on for a month or more. But not many."

"Did anyone survive?"

"Not until they found the cure."

A surge of hope bubbles in my chest. Leelah should totally have led with this tidbit. "What is the cure?"

"I don't know. The king discovered it, before he vanished. The curse vanished with him."

"Vanished? But I thought... Everyone's been complaining about the tithe. If there's no king, whom do they pay it to?"

"The soldiers collect the tithe and send it to the capital —Medea City—where the king's advisors rule in his stead. No one has seen the king since his parents died. Rumor has it he lives..." She turns and angles her face to the high cliff towering over the village. A broken wall of gray-green stone lines the rocky crag, surrounding a ruined turret. Once, I was tempted to hike the hill, but every path I found leading up to the top was blocked by a thicket of thorny vines.

"Up there? But those are ruins." I peer up at it, blocking the suns with my hand so I can see better.

"Are they?" She raises an eyebrow. "Things aren't always what they seem. Rumor has it the king is there, lying in stasis, protected by his magic."

"Magic?" I can't disguise my incredulity. Granted, there are some pretty weird things around here, but... magic? Seriously?

Leelah's looking at me like I'm nuts for sounding skeptical. "Yes, magic."

"I tried to hike up there once," I offer. I wanted to get a glimpse of the sea on the far side of the castle. "There are a lot of brambles with wicked thorns." *But no magic, because magic doesn't exist.*

Leelah frowns like she heard my unspoken doubt. "They say when the king and queen died, the prince came into great power. But he was so saddened by their deaths, he wept for a year. And everywhere his tears fell, the thorny vines grew."

"Wow," I say. "Props to him for getting in touch with his feelings like that. And the thing with his tears creating thorny vines sounds epic. When I cry, I just get a stuffy nose." I'm being snarktastic, but Leelah doesn't seem to notice. "So… if the king is there but *asleep*," I emphasize the word, "who's ruling Medela?"

"The tithe is collected and goes into the king's coffers for his advisors to distribute. He keeps the peace and the sanctity of our borders with his magic, and his soldiers."

"Ah yes, the Alpha guards. My favorite."

Leelah is still staring off at the distant tower. "Once a year, at tithe time, the moonflowers bloom on the vines, and when they do, they guide the way to the king's castle. There is a legend that one day, a beautiful Omega will fight her way up to the palace where he sleeps, and wake him."

"An Omega? But I thought Omegas were incredibly rare."

"Yes," Leelah murmurs. "There may not be any left in the entire kingdom."

"Well, I guess it sucks to be the king, then. Otherwise, that legend sounds like a lovely reverse Sleeping Beauty type situation."

"What?"

"Never mind."

"It's a shame—if this curse does turn out to be as bad as —or a return of—the Red Death, the king would probably have the power to save us."

I bristle. "Then he should do something. It's not right that he's taking tithes and doing nothing to help his people. Someone should go hack down those thorns, and wake him up."

"Yes," Leelah intones. "Someone should." Her eyes

return to me, and narrow. "Where did you say you were from again?"

"Far, far away. You might say worlds away. There aren't many kings left there." I bite back my commentary on defunct monarchies. Leelah looks suspicious already, and now isn't the time. "I need to get home to Matron." I have to ask her if she knows anything about the curse and the cure. She is a healer, after all. "Will you be here tomorrow?"

Leelah looks around and I follow her gaze. People are packing up and leaving the market, their heads bowed and worry lines marring their faces. Across the way, soldiers loom, looking stern as they hurry people along. "I wouldn't count on it," she says. "I guess it depends how the curse progresses."

"The first people to get sick," I say. "How are they doing now? Have you heard anything?"

She shrugs. "I need to ask around. I've been here all morning, as you have." She thinks for a moment. "On the other hand, that might be good news. I'm pretty sure that, if people had started dying already, I would have found out about it."

I slide the package of cakes into the pocket of my cloak. "Thanks for these." Leelah holds out her hand for payment and I drop the coins into her palm. "Stay safe."

"You too," she says. "Tell Matron I wish her good health."

"I will."

In the short time I was talking to Leelah, the market drained almost empty of people. Those who remain are huddled together, whispering about more people taking ill. The knot of anxiety in my chest grows as I clock the stricken, frightened faces.

I increase my pace, my sense of dread growing with every step. By the time I get home, I don't care that I'm sweaty. I drop the baskets on the stoop and burst through the front door.

"Ma?" I hold my breath so I can hear her reply.

There is none. She's not downstairs. But maybe everything's okay. Maybe she's just sleeping.

With my heart thudding in my ears, I race up to her bedroom. The door is ajar. Her room is dark and stuffy, the curtains drawn.

"Rose?" she croaks. She sounds bad—even worse than this morning.

With shaking hands, I pull the curtains back to let in some light. Ma is huddled in the center of the bed, under a pile of quilts.

My relief to find her there is instantly dashed when I see the state she's in. Taking a step closer, I peer at her face and hands.

My heart stops.

Her skin is flushed, her chest rising and falling too rapidly. "Rose," she whispers, and I take another step towards her. "No, child, stay aw—" She breaks into a wheezing cough, unable to finish her sentence.

When she turns her head to cover her mouth, I see it: the bright scarlet blotch on her otherwise mauve cheekbone. "Oh, fuck."

I'M DASHING DOWN THE LANE, MY CLOAK FLAPPING behind me. I don't bother with my hood. Leelah's cottage is closer to the village than ours, further away from the river. I make a beeline to her front door. If she's not home, I'll head back to the market. I have to do *something*.

I left Ma as comfortable as possible. I made her tea, and brought up every herbal salve and tincture I thought might help. She insisted I put them beside her bed, and then ordered me to leave and bar her bedroom door. Downstairs, I paced until I couldn't stand it anymore.

Ever since I woke up on this godforsaken planet, Ma has been there for me. She's clothed me, fed me, promised to help me get home. I have to help her. She has to get better. The alternative doesn't bear thinking about.

I'm hot and flustered by the time I reach Leelah's cottage. Vines have sprouted up in her garden, too, covering her stoop and latticing up her door. What is it with these things? Does no one here own a weed-whacker? I push them out of the way so I can pound on the door. Something crunches underfoot—another greeny-black shoot, covered in thorns.

A growl behind me makes me jump.

I whirl around. An Alpha is standing at Leelah's gate, glowering at me. He's the same one who visited Leelah's booth in the market.

"It's forbidden to pluck a moonflower," he booms. I can understand him. My translator chip must be getting better at picking up Alpha speech. Or I'm getting used to it.

"I wasn't picking flowers." *I was kicking away the thorns.*

"The curse has fallen on this house." He eyeballs me as if looking for any signs of a rash.

I raise my chin, my cheeks burning, but not with embarrassment. With rage. "I need to speak to Leelah."

The Alpha scowls down at me. I guess he isn't used to peasants refusing orders. When your muscles are as big as bowling balls, you probably don't get much backtalk. "You need to leave."

The wind whips around the corner of the cottage, catching my cloak and making it swirl around me.

The guard inhales, his eyelids fluttering. He looks as

though he's scented something delicious. A sigh creaks out of him.

I duck my head to sniff the corner of my cloak. I smell like I've rolled around in a potent body spray, except I haven't. The scent is emanating from my pores.

The soldier is still looming over me. His pupils are blown, turning his irises black.

I don't have a good feeling about this.

The Alpha sways, taking a step towards me.

"Byrol!" another soldier calls out.

The Alpha named Byrol blinks and straightens. He shakes his head a little. "Go home, little one, and pray the curse doesn't find you."

I duck my head and hurry down the side path so I don't have to pass him. Vines line the way. As soon as I'm out of the soldier's sight, I kick them aside. I'm so hot, I want to tear off this cloak, Alphas be damned.

Above my head, someone hisses, "Rose!"

It's Leelah, sticking her head out her cottage window. A scarlet rash is creeping up her bronze skin.

"Oh no. Leelah." I squeeze between two trimmed bushes to approach the window.

She pulls back. "Don't come any closer." She turns her head, revealing more of the rash. The Red Death. "The curse has come for me."

I just saw her at the market. How contagious is this thing? "What can I do?"

"Nothing."

No. "There must be something—"

"Go home, Rose. Stay in, and bar the door."

"I can't. Ma—" I can't finish the sentence.

Leelah's expression softens. "Oh, no. I'm so sorry."

My heart is pounding; my skin is burning under my dress. I have to think. What was it Leelah told me earlier?

"You said the curse ended when the king found the cure. He could help us, right?"

She presses her lips together. Her gaze strays up to the ruins, high on the hilltop. "They say the king has the power to save us," she admits. "But no one has seen him for years."

I turn but the hilltop looks the same. There's no palace, just a pile of gray-green rock and a thorny tangle of scrub bushes barring the way. "And he's up there, right?"

"So people say. But he's asleep. The only one who can wake him is an Omega. His perfect mate."

"But there aren't any Omegas. Is there any other way to reach him?"

Leelah shrugs helplessly. "I only know the legend. The love of an Omega will break the spell that binds him, and bring him to life."

"Okay. Got it. Thanks." I think I saw a Disney movie like that once. As a kid, I used to love that shit.

"It's the only way," Leelah says. "The village council have written to Medea City to petition the advisors who rule in the king's stead. But they don't have the power to stop the curse. Only the king does."

"According to legend."

"Yes."

"But no one's seen the king for years, and the only one who can petition him is an Omega... who doesn't exist. Do I have that right?"

"Yes."

"Great. Sounds like a super efficient form of government."

"I suppose," Leelah says, not getting the sarcasm.

There's another Alpha patrol marching up the road. If I sneak out of Leelah's garden now, I'll be able to get to the river before they see me. "Thank you." I hurry away.

"Rose? What are you going to do?"

"I'll keep you posted," I call, and wave. Pulling my hood up, I dart across the road. I crouch down until the Alpha soldiers pass, then continue down the riverbank.

The cliff topped with the rocky ruins looms up ahead, casting a shadow over the village.

This is crazy. There's got to be more to it than some ridiculous legend about magic and curses and mythical unicorn Omegas.

The king has the power to save us, Leelah said. And at the core of all fairytales is a grain of truth.

"Hold on, Ma," I say, dragging my forearm across my sweaty forehead. "I'm going to get help."

I pick my way carefully along the riverbank, my mind made up. If the king has the cure, I'm getting it. No matter what it takes.

For Ma.

THREE

Rose

THE PATH TO THE CASTLE IS LINED WITH THORNS. I pull my cloak tight as I power up the hill. The heat of the day is fading. I'm still hot, but less so. Moving helps. A strong floral scent is rising from my skin. It's weird, but as long as I don't break out into the rash that heralds the curse, I can deal.

All too soon, the worn stone path is completely blocked by towering tangles of the thick, greeny-black vines. They're a million times worse than the baby tendrils growing in our garden. I duck and twist, fighting my way around them, but after a few feet the brambles are too dense, growing so close together, they choke out the suns.

If Leelah's fantastical story is true, the king's grief created this barrier between himself and the world.

"Newsflash, fucker." I unsheath the giant knife I pinched from the kitchen and start slashing at the toughest roots. "This is nothing a weed-whacker can't fix."

After a few minutes of hacking and sawing, I've made some progress. Sweat is trickling down my neck, and my arm aches from the repetitive chopping motion. I take a moment to massage my sore bicep, and before my eyes, a pale green tendril sprouts from the nearest vine and grows to block my path.

"Are you freaking kidding me?" I push the tiny shoot away. I've never seen a plant grow so fast. This isn't right.

This is magic. A ghostly prickle runs up my spine. "No, it's not," I say. "This isn't magic. There's a practical explanation." Bamboo grows pretty fast, right? *But not that fast,* a little scaredy-cat voice inside me whispers.

The vines crowd around me. When I rise to my tiptoes, I can barely glimpse the castle ruins, bathed in dusky light. The suns are setting. It's already dark in the thicket. What will I do when night falls?

When I turn back around, I'm facing a wall of brambles. The wispy tendril I pushed aside has thickened, and ten more of its brother and sister vines have joined the fray. My little break cost me a bunch of progress, and if the vines keep growing around me like this, I'm going to be trapped.

I struggle, thrashing, slashing wildly at any vine within reach. This is what I get for believing stupid not-so-urban legends.

"Let me through," I mutter, as if the vines are sentient. They're acting more like fauna than flora, by Earth's standards.

The thick stalks knit themselves into an impregnable mesh in front of me.

"Where's an Omega when you need one?" I grumble. "Typical, fairytale bullshit."

After a second to catch my breath, I press on, hacking at the vines.

"Only one true love can break the spell," I mock. "*Twue wuv. Mawage.*" I spout the minister's lines from Princess Bride. "'*Mawage is what bwings us together. And wuv, twue wuv...* Shit!" My knife catches on a thorn and flips out of my hand. It goes end over end then plummets, almost skewering my foot.

"That's more like it. None of those fairytales show the aftermath of the relationship. When you come home and catch him cheating with your best friend." Something twinges in my chest and I rub it away. Am I speaking from experience? I reach for the memory, but it's a shadowy blur. I get the sense that my relationships on Earth—at least some of them—ended badly.

I recover the knife and resume hacking in savage fury. I don't care if I have to weed-whack my way up to the king's door. I'm not letting Ma die.

When my arms grow tired, I stop chopping and just push myself forward, protecting my face with my hands and my makeshift machete. A prickly stalk trips me and I fall, clutching at the thicket to hold me up. My free hand catches on a vicious thorn.

"Fuck!" I shout, and drop into a crouch to inspect my torn palm. The thorn is as big as a railway spike, and sharp as a cactus tine. Blood wells up on my skin. I hiss and squeeze my hand into a fist to see if pressure will stop the bleeding.

It doesn't. Blood oozes between my fingers and drips to the ground. "Fuck," I whisper again. My earlier unease is turning into despair. I squeeze my eyes shut to fight back the tears, and try to breathe. But like the blood on my hand, a tear spills out.

I haven't cried in... I don't know how long. I didn't cry when I woke up on a strange riverbank, on a strange planet, with no memory of how I got there. I don't really miss New York, or scrambling to make rent and find scholarships for med school. Sometimes I wonder what happened to my impressive succulent collection, but that's about it.

Ma is my family. She took me in, and gave me a home. If I lose her—

"She's all I have," I whisper, because there's no one here but me and the vines. I don't have to be strong for anyone.

A sweet scent rises in front of my face. I open my eyes. A flower has appeared on the closest vine. It's shaped like a typical Earth rose but has more petals, which are an amazing ombre hue that go from pink in the center to the darkest, richest wine red on the tips. The smell is delicious enough to bowl me over. And it definitely wasn't there before.

Without thinking, I touch it with my right hand. My hurt and bloody hand. And all around me, more flowers burst open, filling the tight space with an airy sweetness.

Once a year, at tithe time, the moonflowers bloom on the vines, and when they do, they guide the way to the king's castle. That was the legend Leelah told me. The fairytale.

I rise to my feet slowly. Ahead, the stalks part as if a giant, invisible hand swept them back. There's enough space for me to walk without my clothes catching on the thorns—or the flowers. My feet find the worn cobblestone path, and I creep up towards the castle ruins.

The suns are now nothing but a memory shimmering beyond the horizon, but the five moons are rising and their light is enough for me to find my way. Even if I couldn't see, I could follow the rich scent of blooming flowers.

The wind gusts under my cloak, making the fabric billow and tug me forward. The brambles around me are writhing like they're alive, moving and parting in front of me. Maybe that's just an illusion. Maybe this is all a dream.

But when I stagger out of the thicket and crash with a thump into the high stone walls of the ruined castle, I know it's real. I grope along the wall—the vines at my back pushing me forward—and flinch when my fingertips find the massive wooden gate. It's half covered in what looks like moss, but it's sturdy enough, with a knocker set high above my head. Easy for an Alpha to reach but not a human. I go up to my tiptoes, and my fingers graze the rusty ring. Something pricks my palm. I gasp and snatch my hand back. Ugh, I got a dang splinter, this time on my other hand.

Just what I needed. More injuries. I hiss and pull it out, letting the sliver of wood drop.

All hell breaks loose. The ground shakes underneath my feet. I reach out to steady myself, but the gate before me shudders and sweeps open. Afraid, I jerk back from the castle entrance, but the vines behind me writhe and form a net mesh to stop my retreat. The ground rolls again and I surge forward, riding the moving grassy wave like a surfer. I'm pitched through the gates and into the castle grounds. I land on my face on the soft turf.

Behind me, the gates slam shut with an echoing thud.

Oh god. That's not creepy at all. I scramble back to my feet. The good news is, I'm in a beautiful garden, and up close, the looming castle doesn't look half bad. The walls and turrets are a bit weathered, the stone a romantic gray-green that reminds me of Edinburgh Castle back on Earth—but the broken walls and the half-ruined tower I was able to see from the market? Gone. In their place loom high, impenetrable walls, and a whole and intact tower, solid enough to intimidate the most organized medieval army.

It doesn't look like the same castle I see every day from the village at all.

Things aren't always what they seem, Leelah said.

"That's an understatement," I mutter. Instead of more bracken and thorny stalks, I'm lying on a well-trimmed lawn in a lush garden. Whatever the king's landscaping crew is using to keep the vines at bay, it's working.

I'm keeping my knife with me, just in case. I'm not

happy about the gate suddenly opening and closing like a trap door, but the castle looks like less of a horror show than I expected, and now I'm too curious to do anything but keep moving. I find a path and tiptoe through the moonlit garden, careful to keep my cloak from catching on a stray branch. The air is rich with the cloying perfume of flowers, tempered by the spicy scents of herbs. I come across a patch of *dola*. The leaves are so much bigger than the plants that grow in Ma's garden. If she were here, she'd demand to know what sort of fish heads they're using as fertilizer.

Ma. I pick up my pace. I need to get this cure, and get back to her in time. There has to be someone around here, someone I can rope into my quest to petition the king.

I cross what feels like acres of garden, the hem of my skirt getting soaked with dew. The path I'm following leads to a large hedge, a maze of some sort. I wind my way through it and end up on a paved patio. From this side, the castle looks more like a palace, with columns gleaming white in the moonlight. The vines are taking over here, too, overgrowing their trellises to twine up the columns. Every time I pass, the flowers blossom, dumping another wave of floral perfume into the air. It's getting kind of annoying.

My footsteps echo on the flagstones. There's no one around. With the grounds being kept as well as they are, I'm sure I should have come across a gardener—or twelve. Maybe everyone's asleep—but it's barely past dusk.

Another scent hits me, cutting through the intense floral aromas. This one is clean and sharp, like cedar wood or pine. I stop, and breathe deep. A rush of warmth suffuses my whole body, melting all my aches and tension away. Finally, the endorphins from my hike have kicked in.

The sharp scent is strong but welcoming, like freshly baked bread or cinnamon rolls. I follow it past the line of white columns towards a door, which drifts open as I approach. It's clearly not the main entrance, so I'm sneaking in, but maybe inside I'll find someone to talk to. Leelah said the king shut himself away from the world, but who is doing the gardening and keeping the palace lovely? Someone must be.

A gust of wind rushes past me, stirring the flowers. It whips the fallen petals into a mini tornado and spreads them out in front of me to form a long, black-red carpet leading to the side door.

All righty then.

"Magic isn't real," I mutter. The wind stirs the petals at my toes as if in rebuttal. But I catch a bigger whiff of the enticing cedar scent and can't stop myself from hurrying forward, through the door and into the castle.

"Hello?" I'm in a vast space, a ballroom of some sort. There are gilt-framed portraits and shadowy shapes of furniture lining the walls. The scent here is stronger, more concentrated.

The further I venture into the ballroom, the brighter it gets. The light is emanating from the ceiling, where a thousand tiny points glow like stars. Beneath the cedar scent, the space smells clean. This isn't a ruin at all.

A huge statue looms in the center of the room. It seems to depict two figures standing side by side, and one has a hand on a third, smaller figure between them. Two parents and their child? The statues' heads have fallen off, and there's no sign of them.

Something moves in my peripheral vision, but when I turn, there's nothing there. I grip my knife tighter and swallow past my suddenly parched throat.

"Is anyone there?" The wind picks up, tugging at my skirts.

At the end of the ballroom, what feels like miles away and up the stairs, a door slams.

That's not creepy at all. Goosebumps run up and down my legs and arms.

Why did I think this was a good idea? What did I think I was going to do? March up to the castle and find an information booth? Submit a petition?

"Hello? King?" I call. If I keep talking, I won't have time to dwell on my fear. "Hey, King, your people need you." I move past the statue, towards the stairs. Was that just a movement in the shadows on the second floor?

I clench the fist not holding the knife. If there's someone here, they are damn well going to listen to me. "I don't mean to intrude... Actually, no... I *do* mean to intrude. If you're the king, you should do something. Your people are dying. They're saying the curse has returned. The Red Death. It's time to wake up and help them." My voice echoes off the walls. *Help them help them help them.*

I'm gripping my knife so tightly, I can't feel my fingers. Did it just get colder?

Another statue is lying at the foot of the staircase. This one is even bigger than the first—or it would be if it was upright. Someone must have tipped it over. It's broken into several pieces, and chunks seem to be missing. Scratches score the sides like a giant beast ripped at the stone with titanium claws.

Well, fuck. I skirt the statue and chew my lip. Should I explore the second floor?

I take the first step, and a growl reverberates down the stairs. The sound should unhinge my spine, but instead, it releases a burst of heat through my body. My tummy flutters and I gasp, swaying. The cedar scent is so potent now, I can taste it. I can't shake my sense of déjà-vu.

I clock another statue at the top of the stairs. But... it wasn't there before.

I'm panting like I've run a marathon. But not in fear. A

rush of liquid heat throbs through my core and my clit gives a languid thump.

What is happening to me?

The statue moves. The figure's wearing a voluminous cloak and hood and looks humanoid but it's huge, too big to be a regular person. If this is an Ulfarri Alpha, he's the biggest one I've ever seen.

And, judging by the growl, he's pissed. But instead of shrinking back, I take another step towards him. Something about his scent is drawing me in.

The heat emanating from my core spreads up my chest. I lick my lips, swaying up another step. The giant at the top is still. Since he's wearing a cloak like mine, his hooded features are swallowed by shadow. I want to see him. I need to see him. My fingers flex, aching to touch...

I take a deep breath. "Are you the king?"

The figure draws back and lets forth a roar so loud, it brings tears to my eyes. The blood-curdling sound punches through the hypnotic spell of his scent like a bucket of icy water being dumped over my head. A sick, primal terror races down my spine and into my legs.

Without a second's hesitation, I whirl around, and race back the way I came.

FOUR

Bestian

Someone was here. Someone managed to cross my impermeable barriers. And not just any someone...

A female.

I've been pacing my chamber ever since, the light from the moons casting a lilac glow over the flagstones. The distant roar of the waves crashing against the cliffs mocks me like an echo of my own shock at the slender stranger appearing in my ballroom like an apparition.

Who was she?

For a decade, nobody has entered my castle. I've spent countless sun cycles in a deep slumber, safe in my fortress. This place is my retreat from the world. From my people. My kingdom. At times, I wake to correspond with the advisors who represent me in Medea City, but most of the time, I am in a self-induced coma.

My castle and grounds are impenetrable—my magic ensures that. I use a spell of my own making to keep the world out, keep myself in.

How did she get in?

My thoughts are a jumble as I down cup after cup of *blix*. The strong liquor barely takes the edge off but it's better than nothing.

The Red Death, she'd said, in her strange-sounding accent. Could it be true? After all these years, could that Ulf-forsaken curse have returned? The mere mention of it is enough to turn the blood in my veins to ice.

She saw the ballroom, and the statues I destroyed in a rage. The smaller with the three figures—my father, mother, and myself as a child—still stands, albeit beheaded. The largest—my likeness as a grown prince—lies in pieces.

Time heals all wounds. That had been my great hope. Alas, it turned out to be yet another falsehood.

I summon the *whisps* to remove the statue's remains. During my deep sleep, my servants were dormant. Now, for some reason, they are infused with new energy. They cleaned up the rest of the palace, they might as well get rid of the stone debris. I have other reminders of my family.

I prowl to the gallery where my parents' portrait hangs. If the intruder had ventured further in, she would have seen it. Painted by one of the greatest artists on Ulfaria, my parents seem alive once more, their hair lifted gently by an invisible breeze, their eyes gleaming with kindness and wisdom.

It's a knife to the heart.

My mother was a typical Omega—kind, sweet, nurturing. She doted on me, and often expressed her sadness that I was an only child. My father was huge and gruff and stern, and as a youth, I was terrified of him. Now, I see so much of him in myself.

I could have saved them, but I failed.

I was a fool.

With a groan, I stumble back to my bedchamber,

refilling my empty cup for the umpteenth time, wishing I had the power to dull my grief.

It's been many moons since the Red Death came to Medela. A mysterious and terrible curse swept across the kingdom, leaving loss and destruction in its wake. Few were spared.

I searched for a cure, and my efforts nearly destroyed me.

But my parents paid the ultimate price. It is my fault they died.

I sink down onto my bed, burying my face in my hands. The grief is as raw as the first day. I yearn to go back to sleep, to lose myself in the peaceful slumber of oblivion.

Instead, I take a deep breath and exhale slowly, my mind churning.

Could it really be true? Has the curse returned? Is history about to repeat itself?

What reason would that girl have to lie? I hear that last thought in my mother's voice, and she has a point.

Why else would the stranger break into the castle unless she was desperate?

Closing my eyes, I replay the interaction over and over again in my head.

She smelled so sweet, like moonflowers and honey, with an underlying hint of something else I couldn't place.

I couldn't see much of her face, huddled as she was in that huge cloak. She was short, though, even for a Beta. Her accent was strange, almost as if her mouth was unused to forming words, but her voice was clear and sweet despite the desperate urgency in her tone.

She was asking for help, and I...

I roared at her, like the monster I am. She displayed no fear, nothing but curiosity, until that moment. I could smell it: her sweet, moonflower scent turned sour with panic, and—

The thought hits me like a thunderclap and I shoot to my feet, my heart suddenly racing in my chest even as the rational part of my mind is arguing that it can't possibly be.

Her scent was intoxicating. And only one kind of female smells like that to an Alpha.

An Omega.

But there are no Omegas left in Medela.

Can you be sure of that? Again, I hear the question in my mother's voice.

The answer is no. While Omegas are rare, they are not entirely extinct. There could have been one born to a Beta couple—just because I've never seen that in my lifetime, doesn't mean it's not a possibility. There could also be some older ones in hiding, no longer hunted now that they're beyond their fertile years.

I shake my head to clear it. First things first—my people need my help. While I could not save them the first time, I've been given a second chance. I will review my research and, if I can make a cure, I'll send my *whisps* out with it.

In the meantime, I set the *whisps* to continue cleaning the castle. One of them is missing. I wonder if it escaped with the female. That would be another sign of my waning power. But if that is the case, it could prove useful, since I must find her again.

I have to know if my suspicions are true. If she is an Omega, that could change everything. Possibilities I had ruled out forever could suddenly be within my grasp.

I hardly dare to hope, but if Ulf has truly seen fit to send an Omega to me, I know one thing for sure...

I will make her mine.

FIVE

Rose

A GUST OF WIND WHISPERS ACROSS MY FACE, WAKING me. My window must have blown open again.

My legs are aching like I've run a marathon. My arms are hurting like I was gardening all day—which is kind of true. I hacked my way up a mountain, and ran back down with the wind at my back. On my way out of the castle, the gate swung open as if by magic, and the vines behaved themselves. They seemed as cowed by the blood-curdling roar as I was.

Rolling over onto my belly, I pull the pillow over my head, and groan. My mission was a complete failure.

I went to petition the king, and all I got to show for it were some lousy scratches from his overly aggressive shrubbery. Not even a t-shirt.

Was that shadowy, hulking figure the king? Why did no one tell me he was a giant, roaring beast? I've seen plenty of big Alphas at the market, but his enormous, imposing frame was a whole new level of terrifying. His face was in shadow because of the hood, but he was ridiculously tall.

His scent was amazing. The memory makes my mouth water.

But his brutal roar still echoes in my head.

"Fuck him," I whisper, rolling back over and staring at the ceiling. Maybe no one knows the king is like this because he's been lurking in seclusion all this time.

A breeze caresses my face. Something flutters in the corner of my eye. Sitting up, I look around properly for the first time since I woke up. During the night, the vines crept in through my open window and twined over my bed. My room is filled with flowers.

"Are you kidding me?" I push a dangling bloom out of my face, slide off the bed and stomp to the window. Before I reach it, the wind pushes it shut.

That's weird. Wind doesn't typically blow from inside a house. I recall the wind and the strange occurrences last night—before I got roared at.

"It's not magic. There's a perfectly logical explanation."

My closet door flies open and a dress comes fluttering out. It hangs in the air like someone's holding it, but no one is there.

I can't shut my gaping mouth. "How—"

The gown shakes, twirls around, and drapes itself across the bed. A gust of wind rushes around my room, making my bed, straightening the crooked quilt, dusting off my dresser. It even lifts my boots into the air, whips around them in a mini tornado, and sets them down, perfectly polished.

My knees give out and I sag back down onto my neatly made bed.

Apparently, I did get another souvenir from my wasted trip to see the king: my own personal poltergeist.

"Okay. I'm sure there's an explanation for this," I repeat.

The wind ruffles my skirts, reassuringly.

I run a hand over my head and wince. I didn't wrap my

hair last night and my braids are worse for wear. My fingertips catch on something and I pluck it out: a piece of vine with a moonflower bud.

"Can you do something about this?" I wave a hand over my head.

The wind gusts and swirls around me.

My braids unravel and then reform in a second. I touch my head. The rows are perfect. My only issue with it is the flower that got tucked behind my ear. I pull it out and shake it in the air. "No more of these."

The wind whips around the room, gathering all the vines and flowers. The window blows open long enough for the bundle to be tossed out the window.

In three seconds, my bedroom is clear of all plant life.

"All right. Okay. As long as there are no dancing mice."

A sound outside my bedroom makes me freeze.

Someone's moving around downstairs.

An intruder?

Floorboards creak, and dishes clatter. And someone is humming; they sound like—

"Ma," I whisper, and hurry out of my room.

Ma is settling into her usual chair with her tea as I race down the stairs. "You're awake!"

"Of course, I am, child. Unlike some, I prefer to be up with the dawn." She lifts her tea to her face but her mouth is curving so wide, the cup can't hide her smile.

"But... how?"

She nods to the table. "I awoke with my window open, and this potion within reach."

The little wind ruffles the mini-scroll attached to the bottle with golden thread. The alien lettering is neatly scripted but I can't make out a word. My translation chip only works on sound. I'm stuck on a planet where I can no longer read. Not that Ma or anyone in the village has many books.

"I can't read what it says," I say, trying to hide my frustration. "My chip doesn't work on the written word."

"It's from the king." She reaches for it, and I hand it to her. "'If you are touched by the Red Death,'" she reads, "'take three drops of this potion once a day until the rash has disappeared. Every house has received a bottle. If you are feeling well, please give your dose to someone who needs it. Blessings be upon you all.'"

"He did it," I whisper.

"What's that?"

"Nothing. Would you like some more tea?" I turn to the counter but the wind gusts past me. The pot floats in the air, tipping sideways to pour tea into a floating cup.

"Stop that," I mutter, blocking the sight with my body and snatching both pot and cup out of the air. How am I going to explain I went to a haunted castle and came back with a rogue magic wind?

"Rose," Ma says. "Are you feeling all right?"

"Yes?" My cheeks are a bit hot. Not feverish. I'm achy, but that's from climbing up to the castle, and I'm not going to admit that to Ma. "I didn't sleep too well." I carry my tea over to sit in the seat opposite her. Like all furniture here, the chair is Ulfarri-sized, so it swallows my smaller frame. I feel like Goldilocks in the bears' cabin. "Why? Do I look different?"

She studies me, a furrow between her brows. "You look fine. Lovely, as always. But there's something about your scent—"

"Right." I wince and set my tea down. "I got in late last night. I should probably bathe—"

"No, it's not that. It smells nice."

"Oh, that. That's the moonflowers. They're growing all over the place." *Like in my bedroom, up the walls...*

"Yes, I suppose. You've been taking your medicine?"

Oops. I knew I'd forgotten something. "I'll take it right away." I hurry to the cupboard. Better not admit to Ma I missed my dose yesterday. "We're out of *boola* berries." The bowl that holds the herbs I need has nothing but a few sad leaves clinging to the bottom. "And *keeba* leaf."

Ma clucks and makes to rise. "I can—"

"No." I hustle to put a hand on her arm. "I know where I can gather them. You stay here and rest."

She covers my hand with hers. Her wrinkled skin is papery dry and her grip is still weak but she looks so much better already, thank god. "Rose, you must take your medicine."

"I know. I will. Just need to stock up on ingredients. I think I saw a patch of *boola* berries growing beside the path to the market." I settle her back in her chair and push her cup towards her. "And while I'm out, I'll get us some food. You need to eat to regain your strength."

"Child?"

I pause. "Yes, Ma?"

For a moment, she looks small and frail in her giant chair. "Thank you."

She can't thank me for hiking to the castle; she doesn't know I did that. But her gratitude warms me all the same. "Of course. You did the same for me."

"Take your cloak," she calls. The helpful wind beats me to the rack, but I grab the garment before Ma can notice it hovering in the air. Suppressing a sigh, I head out.

The rogue wind accompanies me to the market.

It swoops ahead of me, clearing rocks out of my path. Somehow, it communicates with the moonflower vines, making them retreat before I step on them—which is good, because they're sprouting up everywhere. When I pass, the flowers seem to bloom harder, but I'm sure that's just my imagination. My senses are messed up after visiting that castle—and smelling that delicious scent—not to mention returning with a magical wind, which I've decided to give a nickname: Rogue.

At least it holds my braids back when I crouch to scoop a drink of water out of the river.

I could get used to this sort of treatment.

"Very helpful, thank you," I tell Rogue and it swirls around my skirts, tugging at them like a designer fussing backstage at a fashion show. "But when we're around other people, you need to help... less conspicuously."

Rogue flutters through my braids. I can sense its confusion.

"Less *obvious*. Let's practice. Just pretend you're an ordinary, non-magical wind."

My skirts blow up like I'm Marilyn Monroe standing over a grate.

"Less force," I holler into the gale, and it dies down. "Nice and gentle, a breeze, a zephyr. That's it."

Good thing Ma and I live out past the river. I don't need anyone finding me talking to air.

The suns are bright overhead but it's not too hot, thanks to Rogue blowing gently on my neck. Ma is better—the king quit his roaring long enough to send some medicine. My mission was a success and, best of all, no one will ever know.

There are more Alpha soldiers at the village gate than before, but I duck my head and slip right past them. Beneath my hood, I can't stop smiling.

I'm not the only one who's feeling upbeat. The difference between yesterday's tense, anxious villagers and today's relieved and happy ones is stark.

I start at the bakery then move on to buy some fruit,

casually eavesdropping on people's conversations along the way. It's all positive—there were bottles of potion on every doorstep, so and so is feeling much better already, it's a miracle, Ulf be praised, *et cetera.*

A puff of air around my ears draws my attention to the giant windmill over the tavern.

"Okay," I whisper into my collar. "Go play. But be gentle—"

Rogue rushes away so fast it sounds like a jet in flight.

Seconds later, the old windmill creaks. The wooden blades start to rotate, slowly at first, then moving faster and faster. Folks stop talking to stare at it.

"Well, look at that," the fruit seller says, pointing. "I haven't seen it go so fast since I was a youngling."

I duck my head and mutter, "Don't break it."

The little wind returns to me before I reach Leelah's booth. It blows around my neck and I get the sense it's tired but content. "I'm glad you had fun, Rogue. Now behave."

"Rose!" Leelah waves me over.

"Leelah." I give her a big smile. "I'm so glad to see you well." There's no sign of a rash on her neck or face.

"Yes, the king be praised."

I stop myself from rolling my eyes. "Sure. The king. I guess he came through in the nick of time."

"He did. Because of the Omega." Leelah's expression turns dreamy. "She saved us all."

"Um, the what now?"

"I didn't believe it either, but apparently it's true. The legend came true! An Omega saved us all."

A nearby Alpha snaps his head in Leelah's direction. I angle my body away from him but Leelah doesn't notice. She's too busy waxing lyrical.

"She went to the castle, and everywhere she touched, moonflowers bloomed. When she came to the castle gates, they opened before her. She broke the spell and woke the king from his slumber!"

I run down the events of last night in my head. Leelah's story is one interpretation of things. "I guess we should thank her then."

"That's just it." Leelah's voice drops to a whisper. "No one can find her. She's disappeared. The king has all his soldiers on high alert, looking for her."

Oh, shit. That's why there are Alphas everywhere. I pretend to wipe my forehead and pull the edge of my hood further over my face. "Do they know what she looks like?" My voice is high-pitched. Rogue blows down my back, which feels good because I'm panic-sweating.

"No. The king didn't get a good look at her."

"Oh, good. I mean... that's no good. She didn't leave a shoe or anything else he could use to identify her?"

"A shoe?" Leelah wrinkles her nose. "How could anyone be identified by a shoe?"

"That's what I've always said. Never mind. Dumb idea."

Two Alphas stroll by, looking grim. I bend forward as if I'm inspecting the surface of Leelah's countertop.

"Well," I say casually when the soldiers have passed, "I need to be going. Ma is waiting for me. She's still recovering."

"Let me know if there's anything you need."

"I will." I remember Ma's lecture and pause to ask, "Do you know of anyone selling *keeba* leaf? It's for a tincture. I need *boola* berries and *keeba* leaf. There used to be a patch of *boola* berries along the path but when I looked just now, I couldn't find it."

Leelah blinks. "Who is this medicine for?"

I shrug. "It's just something Ma likes to make." It was my second day here when Ma handed me a cup of moss-green liquid and told me to swallow the bitter brew. *"You must take this every day. For your safety and survival."* She drilled the steps of the recipe into me until I perfected the process of making it.

Leelah has a weird, intense expression on her face. "Those ingredients are rare. I have a little *keeba* but no *boola*. And I wouldn't ask around. Folks don't need to know you're making an estrus blocker."

"Estrus blocker?" I repeat.

"Hush," she hisses. "Not so loud." She shoots a glance at the knot of Alphas standing by the tavern. They're all focused on the windmill which has mysteriously stopped spinning so fast, but she beckons me closer all the same. "Those herbs used to be coveted by Omegas." The last word is barely audible, her voice is so low.

"I didn't think there were many O—" I omit the word *Omegas* at the last second, "of them left."

"In my great-grandmother's generation, there were plenty. And everyone knew that Matron Dia, the healer who taught your Ma, was the one who provided the potion to suppress their heat cycles. To allow them to hide."

I blink. "Why did they want to hide?"

"Because once they go into heat, any Alpha who scents them will go into rut. And once an Alpha is in rut, almost nothing can stop him from giving in to it."

Ah. No wonder Ma is so cautious around Alphas.

"That potion you mentioned, those ingredients?" Leelah continues. "They're illegal. Don't let them—" she risks another glance towards the king's guards, "—catch you asking around for them."

"Understood. Thank you." When I get home, Ma is going to have some explaining to do.

"Attention! Attention, everyone!" A pink-haired older Beta in a fancy blue and gold embroidered robe is standing on a stage in the center of the square, surrounded by soldiers. He holds up a large scroll that looks like a bigger version of the tiny one Ma read from this morning.

"An announcement!" The Beta's voice rings out across the square. "By order of the king."

The soldiers glare at the crowd of villagers until all excited chatter subsides.

"The king has announced a new Queen Covenant. He will visit each village in turn to choose a mate. All eligible females of childbearing age will receive formal invitations." The Beta holds up a second square of gilded paper. "If you receive an invitation, you are to make ready and present yourself in the town square... tonight at dusk." He clears his throat and steps down. The villagers break into loud speculation.

Leelah turns shining eyes to me. "Isn't it wonderful? The king is visiting us. Tonight!"

I lick my dry lips. "What's a Queen Covenant?"

"An old Medii custom. The king travels to each village to meet all eligible potential mates. Traditionally, he would choose an Omega to become his queen. Like now, don't you see? He's searching for his Omega!"

"Great," I say weakly. "I'd better get going." I back away from Leelah's booth, my gaze fixed on the robed Beta and soldiers surrounding him. "Get ready to run," I murmur to Rogue.

It puffs around my ears, whistling down my front to tug me forward by my hem. I get the warning too late. My back hits a solid wall.

Not a wall. An Alpha. I look up into the soldier's familiar face. It's Byrol. He grips my arm, his nostrils flaring —just like last time.

Oh fuck. Not this again.

The wind puffs out my skirts in panic.

"Byrol!" another Alpha calls, and Byrol dips his head close to mine.

"Go home and make ready," he growls in my ear. "We will fetch you just before dusk." He releases me and I hurry away like my boots are on fire. Rogue races with me, making my cloak stream out behind me.

I don't stop until I'm back at the cottage. I burst through the front door, remembering too late that Ma might be napping.

She isn't napping. She's camped out in her chair with a gilded square of parchment lying on her lap and a supremely worried expression on her face.

"Oh, Rose," she says in a broken voice, holding up the king's formal invitation. "What did you do?"

SIX

Rose

Even though I'm twenty-seven, Ma can make me feel like a guilty five-year-old who pinched a cookie. I resist the urge to drag the toe of my boot across the floor. "I went to see the king."

"You *what?*"

When I'm brave enough to meet her gaze, I see her eyes are huge pools of astonishment. Thank god. She's not mad. "At the market yesterday, Leelah was saying this mysterious sickness was like the Red Death all over again. She told me that it happened before, and that the king found the cure. When I saw the rash on your face, I couldn't think of anything else to do."

"Oh, Rose," Ma says again.

I wait for her to continue, to scold me, to ask questions, anything, but instead she just looks at me. I can't read her expression. "Ma?"

"I've done you ill," she whispers.

"What? No—"

"It's time I told you the truth. I've hidden it for too long. A lifetime."

I sink into the chair opposite her. Ma's long, slender fingers are clenched in the quilt covering her lap. I want to reach out and take her hand but she's gazing into the fire as if reading her future there.

"I'm an Omega," she says. It sounds like a sigh.

I blink. "What?"

"It's true. I've been in hiding for decades."

"But... I thought Omegas were rare to non-existent. They basically died out or something."

"Oh, we exist. Yes, birth rates have plummeted but there are other Omegas here on Ulfaria." She attempts a wry smile. "You could say we're as rare as we are fertile."

"Why are you telling me this?"

"Because it's no longer just my secret to keep. Haven't you ever wondered why I always told you to avoid Alphas? To hide?"

"I thought it was because I'm human."

"No. You are different but they would accept that. You must hide because you are an Omega, too."

I laugh. I don't mean to, but... "Ma, no. There's no way I can belong to a subclass of Ulfarri society. I'm a human. From Earth. New York, to be precise."

"I don't know how it's possible, but I know it's true. I am certain. You're an Omega."

I open my mouth and she holds up a hand.

"I know for sure because I'm one," her piercing blue eyes are watching me intently, "and I can scent it on you. You may still be a human, but you're an Omega too. Just as I'm Ulfarri—and an Omega. More importantly, if I can smell it on you, so can they."

They?

The question must show on my face because she continues, "Alphas. Alphas can scent Omegas. It is their nature. Alphas are our warriors. They are born to fight, born to lead but above all, they are all born to find their perfect Omega. To find her and claim her as their mate. And Omegas can do the same. If they scent the right Alpha, they go into heat. It's called the rut in Alphas, and estrus in Omegas. It can last from days to weeks, during which the Alpha and Omega join together as many times as possible with the intent to conceive."

My eyebrows rise higher and higher. Even the wind is still, listening.

"An Alpha in rut can be out of control. Dangerous," Ma says in her most serious tone. "If you and the wrong Alpha scent each other, and he goes into rut, you can forget about getting away," she continues darkly. "He will have you, one way or the other. Not only that, but he won't even think about letting you go."

"Why not?"

"An Alpha's instinct is to breed. Especially once the rut sets in. Since he cannot ever impregnate a Beta—Ulf knows, he won't even go into rut with one—to him, you would be a prize jewel. A perfect mate."

A tingle runs down my spine. I recall that rich, enticing scent. An Alpha's scent. I was scenting the king. An Alpha. And he smelled so good.

But there's no way I can possibly be an Omega, so...

The wind stirs my braids and I snap to attention. Ma is claiming that I'm somehow an Omega, reacting to a biological urge, but I refuse to believe it. I haven't been with a guy in ages. Maybe I'm just thirsty as fuck, and that's why the king smelled so good.

She leans in, gripping my hand. "You must trust me in this, Rose," she says. "If an Alpha claims you, you will never be able to leave. He will keep you forever, or die in the attempt. Do you understand?"

My mind is reeling. This is so much new information to take in. "Of course," I manage.

"That medicine I give you is an estrus blocker. You must take it without fail, every single day. It prevents you from going into estrus, and disguises your scent."

"Leelah says the ingredients are illegal."

Her eyes narrow. "They are, my dear, but most have forgotten. You shouldn't have mentioned it to her. Luckily, I believe she can be trusted. But don't speak of it to anyone else. Ever. We must be so careful. There are too few Omegas left."

"Except you. That's why you knew about the potion."

She smiles sadly. "As an Omega who never wanted to be mated to anyone, I took it every day for all my fertile years. It works, but only if you never skip a dose."

A prickle of panic tingles down my spine. I've skipped two doses now. "What happens if you do... skip a dose?"

"You go into heat. Alphas will be able to smell it on you, and that can send them into rut."

My skin turns clammy and I shiver. "I have no more ingredients to make the potion," I admit. "And I've been called to the village square tonight. One of the soldiers said they would come to collect me just before dusk." I glance at the window. I have a few hours before that happens.

"You must run. Go to the river and hide. They must not find you. Pack some things, and leave now."

"But—"

"I'll be fine." She cups my face. "I will find the *boola* and *keeba* to make the medicine, and come find you. Go to the river where the water can help cover your scent."

Heart pounding, I hurry upstairs. Rogue rushes ahead of me, blasting down the hall and opening my bedroom door with a bang. I follow—and find myself standing in the middle of a mini whirlwind.

"What do I pack? Extra clothes?"

Rogue tugs down three dresses and rolls them into a ball. The quilt soars off the bed and wraps around the makeshift pack.

"Good enough," I mutter.

I stop at my washing bowl to splash some water on my face. I'm so hot. Is it the fever? Did I catch the illness, or am I going into estrus already?

I pull my collar away from my neck, releasing a burst of floral scent like a thousand moonflowers blooming between my breasts. This must be the Omega perfume.

"Get me a moonflower," I say to Rogue, and it races to the window to let in a vine. I pluck a bloom and tuck it behind my ear. Maybe I can fool people into thinking my scent is from rolling in a patch of moonflowers.

Ma meets me at the door with a pack of food and a waterskin. "Go."

I kiss her mauve cheek. "I'll be back. This will all pass, and things will get back to normal."

"Ulf make it so," she intones a prayer. Her eyes are worried.

I make good time, reaching the river with no problems. "Almost home free," I whisper to Rogue. Famous last words.

A sound stops me in my tracks. Some young Ulfarri females are coming up from the river, singing, with bunches of moonflowers in their hair and arms.

It's a lovely sight—except for the patrol of Alphas bringing up the rear.

I stand aside to let them pass, but a hard-eyed soldier motions for me to join the group. Head bowed, I obey, falling in with the ladies. The wind blows a few moonflowers in my direction and I snatch them to my chest, fixing a dopey smile to my face so I look as excited as the others. They're all Betas.

"Isn't it exciting," one of them sighs. She reminds me of Leelah. "The king will choose a bride. Our village is the first to hold the Queen Covenant."

"Fantastic," I reply. She breaks into a wide grin and keeps walking. Like I said, they don't get sarcasm on this planet.

The soldiers close ranks around us, herding us towards the village. Maybe once we get there, I can slip away.

But no, we're marched right into the center of the square, where the market booths have been pushed back to make room for a large platform. The soldiers help each Beta female up onto it in turn. I scramble up before anyone can touch me, and try to make my way to the center of the group so I'm somewhat hidden.

"I need a distraction," I whisper to Rogue. It darts away, blowing through the crowd, ruffling people's hair and knocking back their hoods.

I inch to the back of the platform, looking for an escape route. The soldiers have formed a wall around the perimeter. One of them leans in, his nostrils flaring as he breathes in our combined scent.

I tug my hood over my face and hope the moonflowers can cover the floral musk emanating from my pores. Damn this Omega business. I'm human. How is it fucking possible that I'm going into estrus?

"Look! The windmill!" someone cries.

The wood creaks as the blades go faster and faster until they blur.

"It's going to fall!"

All around me, people are screaming and rushing off the platform. I let myself get swept along and leap off, darting through the crowd.

"Hey!" A soldier grabs at my cloak but I duck into the tavern, racing past shocked servers and customers until I burst out the back door. A group of villagers has gathered there, toasting the king. They turn as one, and someone's ale splashes over me. That's the least of my worries.

Shouts go up behind me. An Alpha soldier is growling, pushing his way through the tavern towards me.

I put my head down and run. Rogue catches up, puffing on the back of my neck as I race down the road.

"Good distraction," I tell it.

The ale does me a favor, covering my scent, but it's mostly worn off by the time I reach the river.

There's another patrol of soldiers nearby. Somehow, I can smell them—a woodsy scent with a pinch of salt and a sour note, like fermented grapes. I wrinkle my nose.

I've almost reached the water's edge when a meaty hand grabs my arm.

The Alpha soldier yanks me up against him.

Byrol.

His eyes are glazed. "I knew you would run. But I scented you first, and you will be mine, *Omega*."

Rogue whips up suddenly, blowing my cloak over his head.

I twist out of Byrol's grip and flee, leaving my cloak behind. The vines part before me and reknit behind me, cutting the soldier off. The little wind caresses my face.

"Go," I tell it. "Get help!"

I don't know what the heck Rogue can do, but maybe it knows better than I do.

It gusts ahead of me, parting the vines wider. Moonflowers bloom as I pass, and I risk a glance back to check the thorny briars are still weaving into nets behind me, slowing the Alpha's advance.

The bracken shakes and shudders. Byrol is hacking at the vines. His muscles bunch bigger and he lets out a roar.

I scramble away, climbing the hill as fast as I can.

It's hopeless. Torches flare in the dimming light of dusk. More Alphas have spotted us, and are coming to Byrol's aid. "Stop her!" one cries. "She's the Omega!"

I'm out of breath and panicking when the same magic as last time kicks in. The ground rolls beneath my feet, a mossy wave carrying me higher up the hill.

I reach the castle walls. The gate is up ahead, but it's shut. *Please, magic, open it, pleasepleaseplease...*

The soldiers are tearing through the thicket, swarming up the hill behind me. I've almost reached the gate when one bursts out of the brush into my path.

It's Byrol again, hacking his way through the thorns. He's bleeding from dozens of scratches. His buddies' torch lights are coming closer.

I back up against the castle wall. Byrol stalks closer, an intimidating smirk on his face. He thinks he's caught me.

A little breeze puffs against my cheeks. Rogue has returned. Has it brought help?

I turn my head, and taste a new scent on the wind. A familiar, heady musk which makes my head spin. It's crisp and clean, dry to the nose, like cedar wood. The king is near.

A bellowing roar blasts the magical castle gates open.

Byrol stands his ground, gripping my cloak. There's a blur, and he's swept away as if swatted by an invisible giant's paw, crashing into the thicket.

An enormous shadow now stands between me and the defeated soldier. It whirls on me—a great, hooded form with glowing green eyes. Its massive shoulders bunch as it prowls closer, its outstretched hands tipped with monstrous claws.

The dry cedar scent slashes through the moonflower

perfume, obliterating my panic, making it easy to breathe again. I should be running. Instead, I suck in a breath and take a step forward, into the shadow of the beast.

A growl rips out of the huge chest, making the ground vibrate.

My heart begins to race. There's a fierce throbbing, then a hot gush between my legs. My knees give out. I collapse against the wall behind me.

Before I can fall, the cedar-scented giant sweeps me into his arms. His next growl sends bolts of desire shooting through my core.

I've never known lust like this before. I'm panting, trembling, burning. This heat is going to incinerate me from the inside out.

The beast's scent washes over me like water on my parched senses. Not understanding why, I press my face against the thick fabric of his cloak and inhale, desperate for relief, drinking in the delicious smell.

"Shhh," he murmurs in a voice barely more than a growl. "You're safe now."

We're moving so quickly, the walls of the palace are a blur. But he's holding me so carefully. So gently.

His hood reveals little more than a pool of darkness. I can't see his face.

My rescuer carries me into a pitch-dark room and sets me back on my feet. I feel drunk. A puff of wind at my ankles unties my laces and loosens my boots until I can step out of them. Is it Rogue? The wind ruffles the hem of my skirts, almost reassuringly.

"Be gone," the beast snaps, and Rogue disappears as if sucked into a vacuum. I'm alone with the massive Alpha.

He leans close, filling my vision. He's so huge, he takes up all the air in the room. He dips his head, crowding me with his massive bulk, and growls. The sound makes my insides quake. A mini eruption bursts through my clit. Golden pleasure suffuses me and I clutch his shoulders to hold myself up.

The growl softens, and so do the shudders in my body. The beast's huge paw skates over my skin. I arch into his touch.

"Exquisite," he murmurs in his deep, dark voice. I want to curl up in his soothing tones. None of this makes sense but my logic is gone, lost to sensation. I feel sounds and hear colors. There's a coil of desperate need building inside me, and everything in me wants to bathe in the sight and smell and taste of the beast.

"What's happening?" I manage to whisper.

"You're in estrus, little one."

Estrus. Cannot compute. I need to tell him I'm human. Estrus isn't my thing. "But—"

"Tell me your name."

I can't resist the command. "Rose."

"Rose." He sounds satisfied. "My long-awaited Omega."

I open my mouth to deny that statement but can only manage a moan. I'm in the grip of something larger than myself, something I don't understand.

And the only one who can help me is the beast.

SEVEN

Bestian

THE ACHE IN MY GROIN IS INDESCRIBABLE. MY HEART is pounding in my chest, my senses reeling with her sweet, slightly tangy scent. And the way her skin feels under my fingertips...

I've read countless accounts of the rut, dreamed of this moment many times, but never thought I would ever get to experience it myself. Yet here I am, holding a real, live Omega.

And she is the most stunning creature I've ever seen. Her smooth skin is such a deep, dark hue, I cannot see her markings. Her rich, golden-brown eyes are framed with the longest lashes, which are currently fluttering in pleasure.

I've never rutted a female, but I've read plenty, and I'm going on instinct as I run my hands over her delicious body. Her ass is firm and round in my palms, and I get a sudden urge to slap it. Later, I tell myself. I want to be gentle with her, at least at first.

"Rose," I murmur. An unusual name for an unusual girl. She's gazing up at me, and when her little pink tongue darts out to lick her lower lip, the last shred of self-control I was holding on to, snaps. Extending a claw, I shear her gown off her perfect body, leaving her completely naked. Now I can explore all of her.

Bending down, I crush her mouth with my own, savoring her taste and the bolt of pleasure that spears me at the delicious sensation of her tongue meeting mine. I retract my claws and my fingers find her hair, twisting into the braids, holding her to me as I drink from her greedily.

My cock is throbbing in time with my heartbeat.

My other hand finds her breast, thumbing her taut nipple. She whimpers against my lips, and I have to suppress a groan.

I kiss her on and on until we're breathless, still experimenting with that plump bud on the tip of her pert breast. I stroke it, tug it, pinch it, listening carefully to her responses. Then I allow my hand to wander lower, over her smooth belly, down, down... until I'm cupping the very center of her. She lets out a gasp when I find her clit and stroke it gently, making little circles, then rubbing up and down, my fingertips slipping easily along the swollen folds of her sex.

She's jerking her hips and gripping my shoulder, making the most delicious mewling noises. Her slick drips into my palm, and I use some of it to paint that growing pleasure bud, stroking her harder and faster for a time before easing off again, testing her reactions all the while.

She likes it slow and firm—that's when she begins to tremble and clutches me until her tiny fingernails bite into my skin.

Suddenly greedy to taste her there, I drop to my knees. Cupping her ass, I hold her firmly in place, pulling my target toward my face. She will have no escape from the pleasure I intend to give her.

With a growl, I lick into her, her sweet slick exploding over my tongue. My cock jerks but I force myself to hold back. As much as I want to rut her, I also want to savor this.

Her clit is rigid as I lap at it, suck it, roll it between my lips. Her hands have moved to my head and now her fingers are clutching my hood, trying to guide my movements.

That will not do. I am the Alpha. I am in control. She will not command me in this. I pick her up and lay her on the bed, before grabbing her wrists and pinning her down. She moans, her hips bucking.

Her scent is driving me out of my mind.

"Be still," I command, and settle a large hand above her mons. Her breathing slows. The orbs in the corners of my bedchamber barely allow any light. It's more than enough for my night vision but she won't be able to see me clearly.

I admire her sleek form as she calms. "Put your hands above your head and keep them there," I say, letting go of her wrists, curious to see whether she will obey me.

Her fingers flex. "I want to touch you."

"Later. For now, do as I say."

I want to roar in triumph when she follows my instruction. "Good girl," I whisper as I quickly move to divest myself of my own clothing. "Now keep them there until I tell you otherwise."

She lets out a little huff, which I ignore. She may not understand why I do what I do, but she will. In time.

Taking hold of her slender ankles, I draw her legs apart and up, bending them at the knees, splaying her open to my gaze. Her delicious pussy parts for me, dripping, and it's all I can do not to ram my cock up inside her right this instant.

Instead I take my time, settling myself back down between her thighs, my tongue once again finding her swollen, rigid clit.

"Oh fuck," she mutters, and I feel her body tense. "Please... don't stop."

I pause, raising my head to meet her eyes. "Don't presume to command me," I warn her. "I am your king."

Her head thrashes back and forth, whipping her braids over her face. I smooth them back and she settles with a shudder. "Please," she whispers. "I need it." She turns her head and licks my palm.

I growl, my cock threatening to burst. I palm her buttocks and lift her hips to the perfect height. I drive my tongue inside her tight little cunt, stabbing as deep as I can, over and over until she's vibrating with desire for me. Only then do I travel up higher to her clit, which I lick slowly and firmly, holding her down with one arm and spreading her pussy lips with my free hand.

"Oh god," she moans, bucking against me as much as she can.

"Don't move," I murmur against her clit. "Just be still, and take it."

My words have the desired effect: a little gush of slick is slipping down between her asscheeks.

I resume licking her, still holding her down and her sex open, bringing her closer... and closer...

Rose lets out a howl and her bud begins to jump on my tongue. I keep licking her until her cunt has stopped clutching rhythmically, wringing every last drop of pleasure from her lithe body.

"Oh my god," she whispers. "Oh... wow."

"Hush." Moving up so our heads are aligned, I lean down and kiss her with all the hunger she inspires in me. I can't hold back any longer. If she wants more when I have lessened the ache in my balls somewhat, she can have it. But first...

As my tongue delves deep into her mouth, I line my

cock up. I'm leaking freely, and she's so wet that it takes a moment to find the right spot. When I do, I have a second of genuine panic. What if I'm too big? I don't want to hurt her. She felt so tight on my tongue.

She undulates her hips, and I can't stop my growl as my cockhead spears her. Ulf, that feels incredible. And that's just the tip.

"More," she whispers against my lips. "I want you inside me. Now."

Bossy little thing. "You presume to tell me what to do? Perhaps I should do the opposite."

"Oh no, no." She arches her back and my cock jerks as if it would leap inside her. "Please... *don't* fuck me!"

The girl is smart—and witty. I allow myself a snort of laughter before I thrust my hips, driving my cock all the way up inside her in one go.

She lets out a moan, her cunt gives a little squeeze.

Satisfied that she's enjoying this, I give myself over to the incredible pleasure of rutting this exquisite female.

Her pussy stretches around my plunging cock like a silky wet glove, milking me as I thrust, sending darts of ecstasy shooting through my veins.

Her little gasps drive me wild but they're not enough. I want more.

Reaching down, I grasp a firm breast, squeezing and pinching the nipple until she gives a cry and I feel her gush around me.

"You like that?" My voice drops even lower than usual, more of a growl than speech.

"Yes," she sighs. "Oh yes."

I twist the rigid nub cruelly. "And this?"

"Mmmh-hhmmm."

"I can tell," I whisper. "Every time I hurt you, your hot, tight little cunt clenches around me."

Her answering gasp is accompanied by proof of my statement. My knot is beginning to form, and I'm perilously close to coming. But I want to savor this incredible moment for a little longer, which is why I'm distracting myself with conversation.

None of the ancient scrolls I read describing the rut even come close to the real sensation. And it is true: Omegas do enjoy being dominated.

"Ask me for more," I demand.

"More, please..."

I direct my attention to her other tit, raking it gently with the tips of my claws—hard enough for her to feel but not hard enough to break the skin.

She bucks beneath me. "Fuck, yes..."

"You're doing well, little Omega."

"I'm not an Omega," she mumbles.

"But you are." I thrust hard inside her, punctuating my claim. "You were born for this. To be rutted by your Alpha. To coat my cock in your slick. You will take my knot and all of my cum. Then I will allow you to rest." I roll my hips, surging deeper. Her eyelashes flutter. "You will sleep and when you wake, your instincts will drive you to make your nest. Then I will rut you again. And again. And again." Her whole body rocks with my thrusts.

She lifts her long, slender legs and wraps them around my hips, trying to pull me closer.

"You're so good," I croon. "You're still holding your arms above your head, just like I told you. Such a good little Omega. Do you want to bring them down now?"

She murmurs her assent and the next moment, her nails are digging into my shoulders.

"Good girl," I tell her. Another wave of her scent assails my senses and I can't suppress my groan as my knot expands fully, sealing her to me. She lets out a gasp as the bulge inside her grows, stretching her wide. "You're mine now, you understand? I'm gonna fill you with my seed... are you ready?"

Before she can reply, I lose control and climax, my impossibly rigid cock jerking over and over again, every pulse shooting more cum inside her, until I'm seeing stars and think I might die from how good it feels. I never knew anything could be so intense.

When at last the pleasure has faded to a warm glow, I lean down and lick the seam of her plump lips, seeking entry. I want to taste her tongue.

We kiss for a moment while I savor just being on her, in her, my cock bathed in our combined juices.

Eventually, I lift my head, looking down at her. Her eyes are glittering in the semi-darkness. "Have you had enough, little Omega?"

"No..." Just one little word, and she still manages to sound both astonished and ashamed.

I chuckle. "Tell me what you want."

When she replies, I can hear the smile in her voice. "I thought if I ask for something, you won't do it?"

"I see you're as smart as you are beautiful," I tell her. "That was just a game, little one. Rumor has it that Omegas find great pleasure in being dominated, forced to surrender... even pain. And from what I've seen so far—"

"I never knew," she admits. "That I liked those things so much. But I guess I do..."

"This is just the beginning, sweet Rose. Now, tell me what you want. Do you want to come again?"

"Yes... but I don't know if I can."

"Oh, you can," I assure her. "And you will. I intend to make you climax until you pass out."

She lets out a little snort of disbelief. "You can try. But I'm not making any promises."

Leaning down, I give her a brief kiss on the lips. "No, you're not. *I* am."

<hr>

I don't know what the fuck is going on with me, when the hell I turned into Miss Nympho, but I do know that I want more of this.

A lot more.

I can't see his face but my fingers explore the ridges and grooves of his huge, solid body. This shadowy beast with eight-pack abs, arms as thick as my thighs, and the deepest, growliest voice that ever existed is giving me the hardest orgasms of my life, and discovering kinks I never knew I had.

As far as I recall, I've never let a guy take control before —in or out of bed. So why does my pussy gush when he pinches my nipple so hard it hurts, when he gives me orders, when he reminds me that I have no control over this situation—or my own freaking body?

Those fleeting, outraged thoughts are cut short when he tugs his impossibly huge cock out of me, the ensuing sharp burn making me cry out... and my clit reawaken. I could swear he got bigger just before he came, and the sensation of my pussy being stretched further, to the point of pain, only drove me closer to orgasm. But I didn't manage to come. I never can, not from penetration alone. Which must be why I'm still so ridiculously, achingly horny.

When he withdraws, it's like he's broken some kind of seal because his cum just starts flowing out of me, rivers of the stuff pooling beneath my butt. And all that does is serve to turn me on more.

"You like my tongue on you?" he rasps, his voice like a knife on rock.

Stupid question. "I do, but…"

"But?" he queries when I trail off.

Oh god. How do I say this to him without my face bursting into literal flames? "Um. I should probably clean up before you lick me again."

His bark of laughter takes me by surprise. "I'll clean you up," he says, and before I can protest, he's shifted us both, moving me with ridiculous ease.

Now, he's lying on his back and I'm on my knees, my sex directly above his mouth. Surely he's not going to go down on me now, after—

His tongue finds my engorged clit, cutting off my protest before I can formulate it. My cheeks are burning with the depravity and shame of it all but holy fuck, the way he's lapping at me…

I drop to my elbows, desperate for the extra support as his huge hands find my hips, guiding me to where he wants me. I'm facing the head of the bed so I can't reciprocate, and have no idea if this is making him hard, but the way he's growling as he eats me out, his tongue vibrating on my clit, tells me he's enjoying this.

And soon the sensations are so insanely good that I no longer care how filthy and depraved this is. All I care about is the way his hot, broad tongue is lapping rhythmically at that swollen bundle of nerve endings that has become my entire world.

The tips of his claws are digging into my hips, and once again, the acute pain is only serving to enhance the pleasure. Then he slides his hands around to find my ass, lightly scratching both cheeks before he uses the pads of his fingertips to separate them, his thumbs spreading me open wider for his greedy mouth.

That's enough for the orgasm to start barreling towards me. I tense up, squeezing my eyes closed, on the verge of—

His tongue leaves my clit then, lapping at my obscenely spread lips instead, and when I give a groan of frustration and try to move so he's back in the right spot, a thundering spank on my right buttock makes me cry out in surprise and pain.

"No, little one," he growls, "you do not get to control your pleasure. I control your pleasure. I decide when you come, and I've decided you're not ready."

"Please!" I whimper, completely beyond the point of feeling any kind of shame for begging. "I am ready! I promise! I need to... so bad..."

He gives me a long, languorous, tantalizing lick, bringing me right back to the brink, then says, "Do I need to spank you to make you behave?"

His words make my pussy clench with longing. There's no way I should be aroused by this threat, and yet it was almost enough to shove me over the edge. The one single slap he gave me felt like a brand. "No!" I croak.

Another lick. My whole body shudders with the pleasure of it. "Here's the deal," he says, almost conversationally. "You're going to stay exactly the way you are. You're not going to move a muscle. You're not going to make a sound. I'm going to lick and suck and tease and torment this delicious little bud—" he illustrates his intent by flicking his tongue over my clit, "for as long as I want to. And when I'm ready to let you come, you will come. But you're not to move. If you move, I'll stop immediately, and I might just find another creative way to punish you for disobeying me—one which you don't enjoy as much."

At this point, I'm fairly sure that I'm going to explode the second his tongue finds my clit again. He still has one hand between my legs, pulling me apart, the other is resting menacingly on my asscheek, which is still tingling from one single spank.

Make that two, I think wryly as he slaps me again. The instant burning sting makes me let out an agonized squeal. "Have I made myself clear?" he growls.

"Yes! I promise I'll try not to move."

"That's my girl."

To my surprise—and dismay—I don't come immediately when he resumes licking me. God knows how he does it, but he knows how to edge me with almost clinical efficiency, bringing me to the absolute brink and then backing off over and over again, until my entire body is trembling with the combination of frustration and the effort it takes to keep still and quiet. Whenever I'm just about to get there, he spanks me again, diverting my attention but ratcheting my lust even higher.

I'm beyond dripping wet. His tongue on me is so loud, it's drowning out my rhythmic panting.

My fingers are clenching the sheets for dear life as I ache and throb, about ready to weep with need.

At last he relents, tugging my lips open further and rubbing his tongue over my clit the way I need it for long enough. It's so intense, I can't stand it. The orgasm hits me like a freight train, bursts of pleasure radiating from my core through my entire, vibrating body. I never knew an orgasm could hurt, but this one does—in the best possible way. The last thing I remember is making a raw, guttural noise that sounds more animal than human, and starbursts exploding in front of my closed lids with each violent spasm of my pussy.

Then everything goes dark.

EIGHT

WHEN I COME TO, IT TAKES ME A MOMENT TO WORK out where I am. My head is thumping, like I had too much wine last night.

But I didn't have any wine. Just cock.

Oh god, the things he did to me... the mere thought of them is enough to make my clit tingle. Shoving the memories aside, I glance around. I'm still in the enormous, fur-covered bed. I'm still naked. My clothes—and the king—are nowhere to be seen.

The room is gloomy but some light streams in from a window slit near the ceiling. It's morning.

Ma will be so worried. I wonder if she's gone to the riverbank yet to search for me.

I need to find some clothes, and head home to her.

Sliding off the bed, I wince as my thigh muscles protest. It's been a long time since my legs were held that far apart for so long, and I haven't been keeping on top of my yoga since I landed on an alien planet.

A small table in the corner holds a pitcher and a goblet.

"

Sniffing the contents, I ascertain that it's *hima* juice, so I grab it and drink deeply.

My pussy feels tender. What a shocker. When the king was—what did he call it?—*rutting* me, I came so often that I lost count. That beast did things to my body that I've only ever fantasized about. And he knew how to plug in to my desires, almost like he was reading my mind. If I hadn't been so distracted with having screaming orgasms, it might have given me pause.

Or not. It was too dark for me to be able to see his face, but his body was perfect: firm and insanely muscular, just how I like my guys. And his cock... holy wow, his cock...

No. Bad Rose. Stop drooling over King Muscles, and work on getting back to Ma.

I can't see any of my clothes or my cloak, so I grab one of the furs from the bed, wrap it around myself like I'm one of the Flintstones, and set off in search of something to wear.

And maybe a bathroom. I smell like wilting moonflowers, a cloying, honeydew scent—and musk. The insides of my legs—and my pussy—are sticky with dried cum. His... and mine.

As I begin to walk, I can feel how wet I still am. Considering I had to regularly use lube with previous lovers, it's strange. I've dated a few guys, a couple of whom I would have called stellar in the sack—at least, until last night—but never in my life has a river of girl juice been gushing from my pussy the way it is now.

The first doorway I find opens to a bathroom. And compared to the modest facilities in Ma's cottage, this is a five-star spa resort, with polished stone walls and floor, an illuminated waterfall running in one corner, thick sheets of fabric that serve as Ulfarri towels, and—best of all—a gigantic, Roman-style tub.

I could have a quick bath before I go home, surely? God

knows I need one. I use the toilet and wash my hands, then stare at the tub, having an extended mental argument with myself.

I need to sneak out before the king gets back. He's not here, he bailed on me, but it's fine. I should be getting back to Ma, to let her know I'm okay. But will another half hour make such a huge difference?

As I dither, something clicks, and a stream of steaming water gushes out of the faucet. Does this stuff work on motion sensors or something?

"Hello?" I call out.

There's no reply.

The steam rising off the bathwater smells divine. With my bare feet rooted to the smooth, cool floor, I stand dumbstruck for the entire time it takes for the tub to fill. As if by magic, there's another click, and the water stops. Is my little friend Rogue back? It doesn't feel like it.

I catch a whiff of my own stale sweat. Fuck it. A quick bath won't hurt anyone.

The water is heavenly as I sink into it all the way up to my neck, and for a long while, I soak, my eyes closed, my thoughts constantly drifting back to the mysterious king and the way my body responded to him—the way it's *still* responding to him, since the insistent throbbing in my groin shows no signs of abating. Though the water is the perfect temperature, my nipples are rigid, aching points, and my lower belly is clenching with desire.

What is going on? Could it really be that estrus thing Ma warned me about? If so, she should have been more clear about just how powerful these urges are. It's been three days since I last took the potion. I imagined that, if I did ever go into estrus, I might feel low-key horny.

This is another level entirely. I just got fucked for half— or maybe all—the night, and right now I'm thirstier than a dude who just did two decades in prison. And I want more than sex. I want...

What *do* I want? It's so bizarre. I'm aching for something but I can't put my finger on it.

With a sigh, I get out of the tub and wrap one of the huge towels around me. I was careful to keep my braids out of the water, but they probably need redoing after the extended sex session.

Too bad little Rogue isn't here to help me.

As soon as I think this, a breeze licks around my ankles, rippling the towel.

"Oh, hello. I missed you." I touch my head. "Can you do my hair again?"

This time, the mini-whirlwind is slower. My braids unravel in fluid movements and each strand is lovingly coiled while my neck is massaged. By the end, my hair is loose in soft, perfect curls, and my skin is glowing with oil. I guess I got the full spa treatment today.

My scalp feels amazing, but when I touch my hair, I find an ornate metal band secured above my forehead.

"What's this?" I pull it out. It's a tiara with silver and gold vines twined around red jewels. They're not rubies—these have a purple and black tint, and flash like diamonds. No gemstone on Earth can compare.

"You gave me a crown?"

Rogue whirls around me once.

Oh no. "Uh, thanks, but I'm not staying." I set the tiara down and the little wind picks it up, making it hover in front of my face. "Thanks but no thanks. Just because I spent the night with the king doesn't mean I'm a queen. I mean, I *am* a queen as in I'm fabulous, but I don't want a formal title." How do I explain a one-night stand to a magic wind? "This was a fling. He didn't put a ring on it."

The tiara floats down to the bath tile with a sad little clink.

That's better. "Is there any way I can get some clothes?"

The bathroom door creaks open. I head out with the towel still wrapped around me.

The next place Rogue leads me to is even more spectacular than the bathroom. It's huge, square, and filled with clothes and shoes—a walk-in wardrobe fit for the most discerning fashionista.

"This is perfect," I tell Rogue. The little wind seems sulky after I rejected the headpiece. It's letting me choose my own clothes.

It's unclear why the king has a wardrobe full of ladies' clothes. I don't judge but it's obvious none of these garments would fit him. In fact, they all fit me as if tailored for me specifically.

I don't want to think about what that means. For the first time in a while, I have all the clothes I want.

I indulge my inner style icon, pulling out what looks like a long piece of fabric in bold fuchsia. Rogue stirs itself to help wrap the stretchy fabric around me. At my instruction, the sheet hugs my body like a tight, knee-length, sleeveless sheath dress. For footwear, Rogue presents me with dark purple ankle boots with a low heel—fashionable, but sturdy, so I can hike down the mountain. There's a gorgeous chunky black wrap that I also take, just in case it gets chilly later. My hooded cloak is long gone.

There's only one thing I'm missing. "Can I have some underwear?"

A section of the wall rolls out, revealing a giant shelf of neatly folded clothes. Rogue lifts up a filmy scrap of fabric. The panties are longer than boy shorts—more like pantaloons. Ulfarri underwear. I pluck them out of the air and put them on. The material is softer than silk and gossamer light, but somehow hugs my ass and thighs. They fit me perfectly.

Of course they do.

Some part of me is supremely satisfied by this. The gnawing ache in my chest is still there, however.

"Well, that's that then. Time to go." I'm going to miss this room and the bathroom. And little Rogue. I know I shouldn't miss the beast, but a part of me longs to get another whiff of his cedar scent.

Rogue opens a hidden door. I enter the secret room, and pause.

Even though there are no windows, it's a sumptuous boudoir, with petrol-colored walls, a thick rug, and long, soft wall hangings made of shimmery fabric. Dominating the space is a padded platform that's three times the size of a California King. The bed. Soccer ball-sized orbs set into alcoves in the walls provide a soft, warm light. The mattress is covered by nothing but a black sheet. Other items of furniture are scattered around but they just look out of place.

The room is pretty, but stark. Almost clinical. I need to make it cozier.

No, Rose, you need to leave. Go home to Ma.

My head is telling me what I *should* do, but what I do instead is go into a weird kind of mania. I start exploring every square inch of the room.

Rogue slides open the mirrored door of a vast built-in wardrobe, and cushions tumble out to scatter at my feet. They're as bright as jewels, in all shapes and sizes. Beyond them, throws, rugs, and sheets are stacked in neat piles under shelves holding rows and rows of candles. I've stumbled into a mini, alien version of Bed, Bath and Beyond.

Perfect.

Not understanding why, I set to work. I need to make this room *just right*. It's an urge as strong as the one I had to fuck last night.

Who am I kidding? The urge I still *have* to fuck.

But the king isn't here, and the pillows are.

Like there's some invisible puppet master yanking my strings, I set about rearranging the furnishings, placing the polished footstool in one corner, a couple fluffy rugs on the cold, smooth floor, and making up the bed. The linens are so soft, I can't stop stroking them. After putting deep mauve pillowcases and sheets on the bed, I add several sumptuous, colorful cushions to accentuate the woven silver comforter. The room is the perfect temperature for me, but I'm still breaking out in a sweat. The huge, heavy, blue velvet armchair is gorgeous, but it can't stay where it is. It's *wrong*. The wrongness of it crawls up my spine, making me want to tear out my hair.

I throw my full body weight behind it, grunting like a wounded animal, trying to get it to shift.

"Fucking *move!*" I growl and let out a little cry when Rogue lifts the chair and positions it where I want it. "That's it," I pant. "Right there. No, a little to the left."

I heave a sigh when the armchair settles into the perfect place.

There's a small table with two chairs, and I direct Rogue to set those up against the wall, completing the look with a gleaming candlestick and shimmering silver placemats.

My pussy throbs the entire time, thumping in time with my heart, cheering me on. It's like I'm being biologically driven to decorate.

My sensible side knows this is ridiculous and a giant waste of time, considering I'm about to, you know, leave, but the inner compulsion is impossible to resist.

This must be what addicts feel like.

I want to fuck. No, I *need* to fuck.

What's the matter with me?

When I've put everything in its place, I retreat to the corner of the room, breathing heavily, scrutinizing every last tiny detail. It's still not right. Something's still fucking missing.

Sudden tears prick my eyes. I cover my face with my hands, fighting back the wave of—what? It's not sadness. Frustration? Maybe. Longing?

What am I doing? I'm back in that mindless state, driven by instinct rather than logic. I'm putting my all into making this windowless room, this sanctum of sorts, my ideal place for sex. I'm making up this bed and creating this lush, cozy ambience for one reason, and one reason only: to get fucked in it.

What was it the king said? *You will sleep and when you wake, your instincts will drive you...*

I'm making a freaking nest.

NINE

Bestian

ROSE HAS NO IDEA I'M WATCHING HER. WITH MY heart thundering in my chest, my cock straining toward my belly, and my soul aching, I stare, transfixed, at my stunning female. When she emerged from the bathing room, she looked regal. The *whisps* reported that she rejected the crown, but it does not matter. My Omega is every inch a queen.

She's busy positioning furniture, straightening sheets, and plumping pillows in one of the many castle bedrooms while one of the *whisps*—the naughty one who escaped my castle spell to follow her—helps.

She's doing just what I predicted. What I could not predict is how satisfying it is to watch her obey her Omega urges.

I'm not an Omega, she protested. But here is proof.

She was still fast asleep in my bed when I left her, one of the furs wrapped around her slender hip, her luscious breasts bare to display still swollen nipples. Small wonder—I teased and tormented those beauties until merely brushing them with a fingertip was enough to make her gasp and shudder.

I've spent countless hours reading about fucking and the rut, and many of those accounts described how responsive most Omega females are to being dominated—and more. To erotic pain. As much as those tales made my cock hard, my logical mind argued that it couldn't be true. That they must be fantasies, written to titillate, not teach.

It seems I was wrong about that, at least when it comes to the exquisite Omega who's currently positioning and repositioning a plethora of cushions across the bed.

I can sense her frustration through the orbs my father had installed to be able to keep an eye on things. Being alone in the castle for the past decade or so, there never was a reason to use them to spy on other rooms, but now I'm grateful for them. As the suns rose this morning and it grew lighter, I had to leave, to work out a solution for my conundrum, but mere minutes without her felt like hours, and I worried about what would happen when she woke up to find me gone.

Now, I can watch over her, make sure she's all right, while I work on my mask.

Only... she's not all right. She's growing ever more frantic and frustrated. Her movements are jerky and tense.

A noise erupts from my chest—a soft purr that deepens and expands. She can't hear it but I'm trying to soothe her.

Ever since I reached adulthood, I've been alone. I've never cared this much about another person. I've done my best by my people, but that was more out of duty and obligation. Aside from brief commands to my councilors, I've barely spoken to another person in decades. And now I'm attuned to one as if her moods, wants, and fears are my own. Is this the bond? But how could it be, since I have not yet claimed her?

These feelings are like moonflower vines, bursting through the soil and stretching towards the newfound light. My world was dark, so dark, but now she is here, shining so bright, I am blinded. She is my guiding star.

I must go to her. She's struggling, and I can feel her distress building in my chest like a physical ache. Tossing down my half-finished project, I throw on a robe with a hood, draw it down over my face, and hurry to save my Omega.

She needs me.

I stride down the corridors, ordering the *whisps* to cover the windows and cut the orb lights. My scent swirls around me, intensifying. Rose's sweet aroma hits me, and I growl.

I erupt through the door to the chamber. My Omega is perched anxiously on the edge of the bed, her face down, her fingers obsessively stroking the comforter.

She looks up, her dark eyes wide, and in that instant I order the *whisps* to dim the orbs, plunging us into darkness.

She sucks in a breath. "Who's there?" My scent must hit her then because she lets out a sigh. "Oh. It's you."

My throat is tight with anxiety. "Little one," I manage, "are you in distress?"

Her hand goes to her mouth and she makes a noise halfway between a choke and a sob.

I'm by her side instantly, pulling her to my chest, stroking her back, growing dizzy from her honeyed scent. "What's wrong? You can tell me."

She shakes her head, her face still buried in the folds of my cloak.

The sudden low rumble surprises us both. Rose starts, then leans back a little to glance at my face before crawling into my lap.

I'm purring. I didn't know I could purr before today. Before I met her. It's instinctual, almost like breathing.

Alphas purr to soothe and comfort their Omegas. It's like a natural sedative.

And it's working.

My mate curls against me in a fetal position, her fingers clenched in my robe, her cheek pressed against my chest.

"Poor little Omega," I murmur.

"I'm not an Omega." Her voice is muffled.

This again? She's so determined to fight her nature.

Let's see if I can show her what she truly is.

I continue to purr and stroke her. Comforting her this way is almost as satisfying as rutting her.

I cannot say why Ulf decided to send this jewel to me but one thing is certain: she belongs to me now. I would kill anyone who tried to part us.

Just the thought is enough to make my purr become a low growl, and Rose's reaction is an instant moan of desire. She moves in my lap until she's straddling me, her hands on my shoulders, her mouth an inch from mine.

I kiss her hungrily, my hand on the back of her head, my cock giving a jerk as my tongue finds hers. I slide my thighs wider apart, spreading her open, until the tight skirt of her dress has ridden up above her hips and her sex is suspended in mid-air, easily accessible. Reaching down, I cup the hot, slick part of her—

Why in Ulf's name is she wearing underwear? I'll order the *whisps* to burn every last scrap of it. Roaring into our kiss, I carefully slide a claw under the material and tear it so I can remove the offending garment. Then I retract my claws and resume growling.

She lets out another moan as my fingers find her cunt and part her lips, holding her open, dragging my thumb over that rigid bud where they meet.

"Oh fuck," she gasps, breaking the kiss and burying her face in my shoulder.

"You like that?" I croon and her clit jumps in answer. "I think you do."

"Fuck me." Her voice is thick. Desperate. "Now. Fuck me now... please."

"Oh I'll fuck you, little one. You were made for the rut. Made to take my cock—and my seed. But first, I want to make you come right here, just like this, all splayed open and vulnerable."

She grips me tighter and her clit leaps beneath my touch.

"You're so ready for me, aren't you? This little bud—" I trace circles over it with my thumb, "is so very hard, and you're making so much slick, it's dripping into my palm. If I took my hand away, you would be gushing all over the floor."

"Nooo!" I can almost taste her shame, but her arousal is obvious. "Please, just—"

"You do not give commands. I give commands. You obey. But I will bargain with you, little one. You climax good and hard for me with your tight cunt stretched wide and dripping, and when I decide you've had enough—when I've milked you to an entire puddle on the floor—I'll reward you with my cock. I'll rut you until you see stars, until your every hole is overflowing with my cum."

Rose started contracting against my hand halfway through my whispered promise, her entire body vibrating with a tremendous orgasm. I keep her little hole spread wide open through every last spasm, my thumb never leaving her pulsating clit.

"That's it, little one, that's my good girl. Don't stop now, I want more. Your slick is splashing all over the floor as you come, it's so fucking hot..."

Her guttural groan turns into a cry of pain as my thumb

keeps moving over her now too-sensitive little pearl and she twists, trying to get away.

I can't stop myself from grinning. My cock is so hard, it aches, but the way she responds when I tease her is like nothing else I've ever experienced. I'm so attuned to her that her pleasure is like my pleasure.

And I fucking love pleasure.

"Nuh-uh, you're not going anywhere," I say, lightly slapping her sopping sex. "I'm not done yet. An entire puddle, I said. And don't bother pretending you're not enjoying this. Your cunt doesn't lie." I readjust my grip, spreading her labia again before resuming my stimulation of her clit with my thumb. My free hand is gripping the back of her neck, pinning her in place. "I love how your tight hole tries to contract but it can't, not when I'm holding it open nice and wide. Just like how you try to get away but you can't, little one. All you can do is hang here with your dress rucked up, your gorgeous bare ass on full display, and drip onto the floor as I pleasure you."

Her face is still buried against my shoulder, and even through my robe, I can feel how hot her skin burns.

"Poor little Omega," I repeat, and this time she doesn't argue. She's too far gone.

I increase the pressure on her clit slowly, slowly... until she gives a garbled cry and shudders, her pussy snatching rhythmically at my fingers.

"Good girl, let it all out," I coax her, "Ulf, that's so hot. You're so wet, making such a mess. But it's good. You know you need to be nice and slick so I can fit my big cock all the way up inside you..."

She's chanting now, her words muffled but still distinct: "Fuck me, fuck me, fuck me..."

My cock is about to burst. My canines ache, and I'm blasted by an overwhelming desire to claim her fully, to sink my teeth into the soft flesh of her neck. It would be so easy. I would just need to turn my head, and—

No. Gripping the hair at the back of her neck, I tug her head back so she's forced to look at me. At the same time, I slide three fingers up inside her wet heat, finding that rough spot that drives her crazy. Sure enough, her eyes glaze over instantly.

"Look at me," I command, still growling, "I want to see your face as you come all over my fingers. And then, when you're done, I'll replace them with my cock. But first, I need to wring every last drop of slick out of you—force you to ride out every last spasm—to make room for all the cum I'm gonna shoot up inside you—"

I'm interrupted by Rose's scream of ecstasy as she flies over the edge yet again, her violent orgasm so strong, she almost takes my fingers off.

When at last she slumps, sated, against me, I bring my slick-soaked hand to my mouth and lick it, lapping up her musky, sweet juice. It's intoxicating.

If I don't get inside her right now, I will die, I'm sure of it.

"Now I think you're ready for me," I croon, freeing my throbbing cock and shifting her until the tip is lined up with her slick hole. "Still want more?"

"Yes," she whispers, hoarsely. "Please."

I lower her slowly, impaling her inch by inch, my heart hammering at the intense, delicious sensation. My knot forms almost instantly.

I want to come but I want to savor this some more, first. "Ride me, little one," I coax but she's struggling, limp from too much pleasure. So instead I pump my hips, holding her in place like a puppet, driving in and out of her harder and harder until my knot expands all the way and I come with a roar.

Only when the flashes of white light stop dancing behind my eyelids do I realize what I roared when I climaxed.

It was her name.

Rose.

My fated mate.

My queen.

TEN

Rose

MY LIMBS ARE HEAVY, TINGLING. THERE'S A RAW ACHE between my legs, and I feel drunk. How long have we slept? It feels like years. The huge Alpha behind me is holding me tightly, one massive arm slung over my hip, his breath hot on my shoulder. Is he still asleep? I turn my head to check.

"Look away," he growls, and I obey instantly.

How does he have this effect on me? I scowl at the wall.

"Forgive me, Rose," he says at length. "I should not be so harsh."

I try to stiffen but I'm too relaxed. He fucked the stress out of me. Which is another conundrum—why was I so stressed in the first place? "I don't know what's happening to me," I mutter.

"You are in estrus, Omega. The records describe it as being overwhelming, especially the first time."

I huff. I wish he wouldn't keep insisting. "I'm not an Omega."

He plays with my curls. I should pull away, but his

touch makes me shiver. "If you are not an Omega, why do you take my cock so well?"

I suck in a breath as my clit gives a slow, languorous thump. I've just been fucked to within an inch of my life, and already I want more. "Don't start again."

"Why not?"

I wrench myself out of his embrace and wriggle away.

"Where are you going?"

"I need a shower."

"Later." He pulls me back into his arms and gives the back of my neck a lingering lick. "I enjoy you covered in my scent."

"I don't." It's a lie. I love his scent. I want to lick him back.

Ugh.

I squirm away again and slide off the bed. Wobbling on strained thighs, I wrap my dress around me, doing my best to get the fabric to drape the way Rogue got it to before. No point in looking for my underwear. He tore it off with his claws.

God, if anyone had told me I'd be even thinking *any* of this shit just six months ago—let alone experiencing it—I would have suggested they get a mental health evaluation.

"Omega," the king murmurs, and starts to purr.

I shake my head, but don't deny it aloud. I want to argue with him, but I'm too busy fighting myself. The formerly perfect bed I spent so much time and effort on is a mess, and must be put to rights.

I pick up a pillow and hum in satisfaction. It's redolent with both my and the king's combined scents.

"What are you doing, my little moonflower?"

"Nothing." I prop more cushions on the bed around the giant shadowy form. "I can hardly see in here. Can you turn on the lights?"

"No."

I drop my remaining pillows. "Why not?" The bed is a huge pool of darkness. Today his cedar scent is sweetened with a touch of honey.

The giant on the bed rises to a sitting position. I can make out that much in the gloom. "It is my will."

I have an insane desire to throw a cushion at him. "Your will."

"Yes."

"Fuck your will." I fold my arms across my chest. "I don't even know your name."

"Is that why you are upset?" The rumbling in his chest increases, instantly soothing me. Which is annoying. "You may call me Bestian."

"Oh, thank you, Your Majesty. Do you keep all your subjects in the dark, like mushrooms, or am I just lucky?"

"I do not allow anyone to see me, Rose. And none of my subjects can pass the magical barrier I've conjured around my castle. You should not have been able to penetrate it so easily."

"That's what she said," I reply automatically, but my brain is scrambling. *Magical barrier?*

"Come, now. A truce." The orbs in the corners of the room begin to glow just a little. The king stretches back out on the bed, his hood still hiding his face.

I want to go to him, so I make myself take a step back, and step on a cushion. It seems like *all* the decorative pillows got tossed around during our fuck fest. I gather the remaining ones into my arms and start arranging them on the bed.

The king is silent for a while, watching me work. Then, "Why do you believe you are not an Omega?"

"Because I'm not. I'm human."

"What is a *hew-man?*"

"I'm from another planet. I don't know why I'm here." I fuss with a fluffy pink cushion until it's just right.

What am I doing? I should be packing up, leaving, but I can't until this room is set to rights. It's a compulsion.

"Shall I summon the *whisps* to help?" Bestian asks.

"No," I growl, karate-chopping a pillow the way I've seen decorators do on HGTV. "I want to do it myself."

"Why? What are you doing, little Rose?"

"I'm not little." I smoosh two pillows together. I need the combination of our scents to be balanced perfectly. "I'm fixing what needs to be fixed."

"Nesting," he says with satisfaction. "Because you are an Omega." He puts his hands behind his head, a mountain in repose. "Ulf has blessed me. All the kings on Ulfaria are scrambling to find Omegas, and meanwhile one simply walks into my palace, demanding an audience."

Something tugs at my thoughts. *Ma. Home.* How could I have forgotten her? "I need to go," I mutter.

The Alpha snaps to attention, his purr becoming a deep growl. My core flutters.

"No. Don't do that," I whisper. His scent, his voice, his growl—they're all a siren call I can't resist. I rock forward, taking a step toward the bed before I can stop myself.

"Why not, little Omega? Are you unable to control yourself?"

I take another step, and Bestian growls louder. I'm seconds away from crawling onto the bed and attacking him. Since when am I so sex crazed? True, I've had a long dry spell since arriving on Ulfaria, and for all I know, I came to this planet on the tail end of a sex drought, but this is intense.

It must be that estrus thing.

My stomach rumbles loudly.

Bestian stops growling at once. "You need sustenance. I have failed you."

"Sustenance?" Who talks like that? But the king clambers off the bed, and the room shrinks with his bulk.

"I will leave you to settle. You will eat and drink and settle. When you have finished your nest, I will return." His thick, long fingers caress my face, and he is gone before I can protest.

The nerve of him.

The door clicks open and Rogue whisks in. The glowing orbs brighten and the room is flooded with light. The little wind brought a tray of Ulfarri delicacies, including my favorite sweet cakes. The air flow freshens the room, and as I watch, Rogue tugs at the silvery comforter until it's military-grade neat.

My hollow stomach urges me towards the food. I want to eat and drink and nest. Just like the king ordered.

So I will. But he won't find me here when I'm done. Yes, everything here is magical and ethereal and too damn perfect. And yes, the sex is beyond anything I ever could have imagined. But none of this is real. Participating in the king's fantasy that I'm his *fated mate*, somehow born to be his queen was a fun diversion, but it's just that. A *fantasy*. And I don't like the way my thoughts, feelings, and body are constantly at war with each other when I'm around Bestian. He has way too much power over me. Not to mention the most important thing: I need to let Ma know I'm okay.

I've made up my mind. I'm going to leave.

And this time, I'm not going to let the irresistible Alpha stop me. No matter how much he growls.

My lovely Omega eats with a hearty appetite—except for the sweet cakes, which she slows down to savor. She wraps several in a napkin. Hoarding food? She has been living like a peasant. I must make sure she understands that food is plentiful here.

I order the *whisps* to deliver more cakes, and turn to the jumble of scrolls on my desk. I've collected every Omega-related treatise from the library. By the time I was born, Omegas were increasingly rare—not just in our kingdom, but all Ulfaria. My mother was one of the few remaining. My father found her during the Queen Covenant, and he had to search all the villages the length and breadth of Medela to find her. In those days, the Queen Covenant was called the Omega Covenant. Then, due to the waning Omega birth rates, it was renamed. I was the first king of Medela who faced having to take a Beta to wife. A Beta queen might have provided me with companionship and sex, but there would be no heirs to further the line—she would be nothing more than a glorified mistress. So I resigned myself to a life spent alone... until Ulf deemed me worthy of an Omega.

Why this gift after so many years of suffering, I do not know. I can only strive to be worthy of her. Thus: the scrolls. When I was young, my father made me study everything that was known about Omegas. That is how I know about rutting, knotting, slick, and estrus. That Rose would respond to my growl, domination, carnal pain, and my purr. But there is still much for me to learn.

Why was she able to broach the magical barrier between me and the rest of my kingdom? It is written that Omegas have their own gifts. All kings have power that connects them to their land. I inherited mine from my father. But my mother also had the gift of healing. Her magic complemented my father's—increased it. Together, they were a formidable force. Until the final spell destroyed them.

I stop my thoughts before they stray too far down that dark road.

My parents are gone, but Rose is here. I must study so I can return to her. Once she has rebuilt her nest to her satisfaction, she will be desperate for me to rut her in it. The thought makes my lips curve up. The muscles of my face are aching from the unfamiliar movement. I haven't smiled this much in a long, long time.

A *whisp* rustles the scrolls on my desk.

"What is it?"

The orb I'm using to watch my Omega floats closer. The image reveals the nesting room made up neatly, with columns of pillows stacked in artful piles. All the sweet cakes from the second plate have vanished, too, leaving only crumbs.

But the room is empty.

My Rose is gone.

ELEVEN

IT TOOK A LITTLE CAJOLING TO GET ROGUE TO LET ME out of the nesting room. First, I claimed I had to go to the bathroom—which was true. Washing my face had the added benefit of clearing my head. I held my packet of smuggled sweet cakes to my nose to ward off Bestian's delicious scent. My kryptonite.

The next hurdle was finding a window that looked out over the garden. But when I made a fuss about wanting to pick a moonflower, the little wind relented and guided me to a balcony. And what do you know, one side was covered in moonflower vines, the perfect thickness for climbing.

The suns have just set and the moons are clambering up into the sky. My gut feeling was right—we did sleep for ages. Rogue tugs at my hair and wrap dress as I stride down the path dividing the manicured flower beds. "Nothing personal," I tell it. "I need to get home to Ma. She's probably worried sick."

The little wind blasts my curls back and I break into a jog, winding my way through the hedge maze. The air is heady with the scent of moonflowers and a touch of salt. The castle overlooks the coast, and the roar of the surf is faint, but ever present in the distance.

Up ahead, the wall looms in the darkness. When I reach it, I'll have to figure out how to open the gate.

I'm almost at the end of the maze when I'm hit with a burst of cedar scent. A huge shadow detaches itself from the hedge wall and blocks my way.

"If you wanted to take a stroll in the gardens," Bestian says in an amused tone, "you only had to ask."

Fuck, fuck, fuckity fuck.

The hooded king towers over me. I squint up at him, but his head and upper torso are in shadow.

I flick a stray curl out of my face and try to act casual. "Maybe I wanted to walk alone."

"You will never be alone again, Rose. Or have to go without." He reaches out and plucks the bundle of sweet cakes from my hand. "You have only to ask, and my servants will bring you hundreds of these."

"Servants?"

"The *whisps*. You are quite comfortable with one. It followed you all the way home after your first visit. Even though it had strict orders not to leave." His tone turns sharp.

The little wind in question is cowering behind my ankles.

"Don't be mean to it," I say. "It helped me. I would've been Alpha bait without it."

A menacing growl erupts from his broad chest. "You should never have been in such danger."

"I wouldn't have been if you Alphas were able to control yourselves."

"It is the way of an Alpha to lose control around an

Omega. Perhaps even more so now that Omegas are so rare."

"Everyone keeps saying that, but why? Why are they so rare?"

"If I knew, little one, I would tell you." His voice softens the way it does when we're in bed and he's whispering filthy nothings in my ear. I hate the way I love it. "I've spent my life trying to find out why." His huge hand settles on my back and I let him turn me. He's too big—I have no choice. "Come now. Back inside."

"Can we walk a little?" I lean back against his palm. "The moonlight is so nice." And the more I explore the grounds, the easier it will be to find an escape route. That's my real purpose, even if everything inside me sighs with contentment whenever the king's around.

Bestian pauses. "Very well. We will walk. And you will explain to me why you do not think you are an Omega."

I roll my eyes, glad I'm facing away from him. How many times do we have to go over this? Is the concept really so hard to grasp? I'm a human being. From a completely different fucking planet. Therefore, I can't be an Omega, and I can't be in estrus, period.

Then why do you react to the king the way you do? Why does a single look from him, or touch—not to mention his ridiculously delicious scent—turn you into a helpless bundle of need and make you forget everything but him?

The whispering voice of doubt in my head lists so many questions, but the answer remains the same:

I. Don't. Fucking. Know.

I wonder if I'll ever be able to figure it out.

Rose turns and tilts her head up to me. Is she trying to see my expression? Before I raced to intercept her, I wove a spell to mask my face, but it is incomplete. The curse that marred my features is resistant to magic.

My spell obscures the worst of the damage. The growing dusk and my hood do the rest.

"I know I'm not an Omega. So I don't understand why I'm reacting the way I am. Some sort of psychosomatic response? Delayed trauma from waking up on an alien planet?" She's half talking to herself, and I'm pleased. I never thought I'd possess an Omega, much less one who can match me intellectually. The *whisps* told me she was in training with a healer in the village. Perhaps Rose can develop healing powers, like my mother.

"I'm human. I can't be an Omega."

I guide her through a hedge exit. Her muscles tense under my touch, but she obeys. Her acquiescence pleases me, but her impending disobedience intrigues me even more. I've never met anyone so determined to counter my will.

It's exciting.

"A few summers ago, I would have agreed with you," I tell her. "But in recent past, there were instances of Ulfarri kings finding their Omegas. The Wanderer King and the Golden King, as well as the Hunter King have found their mates. In each case, the Omega was like you. Human."

She stops walking and sucks in a breath. "That's impossible."

"Is it? How did you come to be on Ulfaria?"

"I don't know."

"In the other queens' cases, they were brought through a portal and given a serum to turn them into Omegas."

She leans forward, placing a hand on her stomach.

"Rose? Are you all right?"

"Are you telling me... not only was I abducted by aliens, but they also gave me a serum to turn me into an Omega?"

"That is my theory."

She rubs her chest absently. "I still *feel* human."

"You are. Your slight stature and features are similar to those of the other kings' Omegas. But, like them, you also display Omega traits." She's still staring into the night like it holds all her answers. I brush my fingers over her gleaming curls. "It is a gift."

"Not to me. I'm the one who got transformed."

"Is it so unsettling?"

"Unsettling? That's one word for it." Her sweet scent carries a whiff of ash. Alarm surges in my chest, triggering my purr.

I stoop and swing her up into my arms. Her neck stiffens. The rest of her melts against me, molding to my chest until her entire body is vibrating with my rumbling purr. Her perfume turns sweeter and thickens to nectar on my tongue.

"What are you doing?" She sounds drowsy from my purr's soporific effect.

"There is something I want to show you." Holding her close, I set off, marveling at how perfect she feels in my arms. But then, I shouldn't be surprised.

She belongs in my embrace.

She belongs to me.

My mind is at war with my body. I hate that the king is carrying me, that he presumed to pick me up without asking. I hate the thrill that prickled under my skin when he swung me into his massive arms. I hate how I'm pressing myself against him. I hate the rumbling purr and how it makes my entire body relax like I just had a two-hour massage.

I hate how the evening air is soft and perfumed with moonflower scent. I hate how Bestian is carrying me like I weigh nothing. I hate the gorgeous five moons and how that little voice in my head whispers, *Isn't this romantic?* as we travel through the gardens together.

But most of all, I hate how much I'm loving this. All of it.

We go through a covered walkway, and when we emerge, we're bathed in lilac moonlight. Even at night, this place is stunningly beautiful.

It's annoying.

"Do the *whisps* do all the landscape maintenance too?" I ask.

"Of course."

"How do they work?"

"Magic."

I realize I'm absently stroking the emerald green markings on Bestian's chest and snatch my hand back. "Magic isn't real."

"Isn't it?" He sounds amused. "I'm devoted to learning. I've studied magic all my life."

"Where does it come from?"

"Members of my family all have innate powers, but the bulk of the magic I use comes from the kings' symbiosis with the land."

"Ask a stupid question," I mutter.

"There are no stupid questions, little Omega."

"And now you sound like my seventh grade science teacher. Except for the Omega part." I snuggle closer to him, not because I need to, but because he's warm and the night has a chill that penetrates my wrap.

"Settle, little one. We're almost there."

Something's glowing up ahead. Bestian carries me through a massive archway, towards the gurgling sound of running water. Smack bang in the middle of a square courtyard is a frothing fountain surrounded by rows upon rows of lights.

No, not lights. Flowers.

The five moons are out, and they're bright, but there's no way they're giving off enough light to be making those flowers glow in the dark like that. Each bloom glows as if it has a miniature lightbulb inside it.

The king lets me slide out of his arms. I hurry over to the nearest blossom, stroking its soft petals. "These look like moonflowers."

"They are. That's how they got the name."

"But..." I look up at the palace, where more vines cover the columns. Sure enough, there are dots of light glowing within the profusion of thorns. I must have missed them when I was trying to escape—or chalked them up to hidden lights. "I've never noticed them glowing before."

"They don't glow until a few days after blooming." Bestian settles his huge bulk onto the bench. "You can pick one, if you like."

"No." I don't want to destroy a single one. "But... what would happen if I did? Would it stop glowing?"

"Not for a long time. My father planted this garden for my mother. We used to have bowls full of moonflowers in the ballroom."

There's a wistful tone in his deep, gravelly voice. His parents died, right? That's what Leelah said in the marketplace. "The old king and queen?"

"Yes. This was their autumn home."

"Oh, autumn home?" I roll my eyes. "Did you have one for every season?"

"Yes."

"Of course."

He leans forward. I can't see his face but his eyes are gleaming. "Is that why you wish to leave? You resent my great wealth?"

"I resent that you live in luxury while your people suffer."

"My people are well cared for." He waves a hand. "My advisors see to their needs."

"Your people were falling ill and dying." I turn away from the flowers, my fists clenched at my sides. The king is so much bigger than I am, but when I think of Ma at death's door, I want to slap him. "That's the whole reason I came up here. I never would've come here otherwise."

"And I am very glad you did." His purr has deepened into a growl.

I grit my teeth, fighting the wave of arousal that surges in me. Everything in me aches to cross the distance between us, to go to him. *Come on, body, I'm trying to have a conversation about wealth inequality.*

"I sent a potion that will stop the spread of the curse," he continues.

"Not quite universal healthcare, but okay."

"You are getting upset, Omega."

"Stop calling me that." I turn away from him, focusing on the flowers once more. I inhale deeply, but get a huge whiff of the king's scent along with the floral perfume. My shoulders relax. "I need to get back to Ma," I whisper, mostly to remind myself. Fuck, why is it so hard to focus on anything but Bestian?

"Rose." He extends a giant hand tipped with black claws. "Come to me. I promised you a truce. Let us talk as equals."

It's a trap! But until I can escape, I might as well find a way to reason with my captor. "Stop growling," I say, and the sound cuts off like he flicked a switch.

I take a small step closer to him.

"Look, Your Majesty—"

"Bestian," he corrects me.

"Bestian." My body sighs at the rightness of his name on my lips. "I don't trust you."

"I know, little one. It pains me. Come to me, and let us come to an accord."

I'm already taking more steps towards him. I tell myself it's because I want answers, but it's really because I want to be close to him. I want to wrap myself up in his scent.

As soon as I'm close enough, he catches my arm and tugs me down to him. Instead of making room on the bench, he positions me on his broad lap, facing outwards.

"Good girl," he croons in my ear, the same way he does in bed. A rush of heat floods my face. Another wave of his scent rolls over me—rich pine needles, freshly brewing coffee, dark chocolate, the dry cedar—and I bite my lip as a dart of desire hits my clit. *No. Bad Rose. Focus.*

"I want to face you." I wriggle, and his arm tightens around my middle. "I don't know what you look like."

"And you never will. I am not... fit to look upon."

Why not? He sounds sensitive about the subject, so I say, "You could let me be the judge of that."

"Perhaps." He sounds amused.

This is stupid. He wants to speak to me as an equal, but it's clear he doesn't think I am one. I get the sense it has nothing to do with my social or alien status. It's that Alpha/Omega bullshit. "What do you want from me?"

"I've told you from the first. You are my Omega. My mate. We were born to be bonded. Two bodies, one soul."

I snort. "Unlikely, since I'm not from here."

"Ah, yes, your human status. Ulf is all-powerful. He found you, and helped you traverse the galaxies so we could be together."

"Fine. Maybe he did. But I don't want to be your mate," I say, even as I melt back into his chest. It feels right, being this close to him.

At least he's stopped growling. If he starts purring now, I will punch him.

"You lie, Omega." His voice rumbles through me, as effective as a purr. Dammit. "I don't understand. Why fight so hard to deny your true nature?"

"Some of us have responsibilities." *Unlike you, oh, king, who holes up in your magical castle and leaves your kingdom to rot.* "I'm not going to ditch my only family because of some epic sex." *Besides*, I add silently, *that* true love forever *bullshit isn't real.*

"Epic sex?" Again with the amusement.

"You know we're compatible," I mutter, and try to ignore how a fresh wave of my scent rises to mingle with his.

"I will send the *whisps* to check up on Matron—a mercy, since she was concealing an Omega from me. By Ulfarri law, she should be punished, not rewarded."

A cold finger of dread travels down my spine. "She didn't know."

"Did she not? A healer with extensive knowledge of Ulfarri physiology? I find it hard to believe she did not scent your Omega status from the first."

"But I'm not Ulfarri. I'm human—"

"Not any longer. As much as you deny it, you are more

Omega than human." He cuddles me closer. "Perhaps a part of you is reluctant to accept it. I will allow you time to grieve."

"Oh well, thanks. How gracious of you."

"I understand grief, little one."

That shuts me up. There's so much about him I don't know. "Your parents?"

"Yes."

I keep my voice level, fighting to remain logical. "So you understand what Ma means to me. She saved me, took me in. No questions asked. She's the reason I survived here, in Medela." I turn in his lap, not facing him, but letting him see my profile. I keep my eyes fixed on the fountain, and my tone mild. "What do you think your Alpha soldiers would have done if they had found me?"

A menacing growl bursts out of Bestian's chest. I jump but can't escape his imprisoning arms. Even if he didn't have iron muscles, I don't want to leave my cozy perch. The heat from his body makes me drowsy.

"It is not worth thinking about," Bestian says. "Ulf preserved you for me."

"If he did, he used Ma to do that. She clothed me. Fed me. She's my family."

"Do you not have family back on your planet?"

"No. I was all alone." That much, I do remember. I was a model, working to pay my way through a bachelor's and ultimately medical school, but all alone. No one in my tiny apartment but me—and a hundred potted plants. "Ma's cottage is my home now."

Bestian's arms tighten around me. "The palace is your home now."

"No."

"Yes. You have set the challenge, little one. I will do anything to convince you."

"You have your work cut out for you." I yawn.

Instantly, he's on his feet, striding to the palace. "My Omega is tired. I have not cared for you as I should."

He makes it sound like I'm his pet.

"I want to keep talking," I say stubbornly.

"I will talk with you for as long as you wish. After you've slept."

I fight to keep my eyes open but as he ducks through an archway, his purr roars to life.

After a few seconds, I'm lost to the world.

TWELVE

Bestian

My Omega is sleeping. There is so much for her to know. About me, about herself. About us. Reading the histories of Omegas will only do so much good. She is part human, no matter how much I want to deny it.

I wish to deny her human side, she wishes to deny her Omega dynamic. I wish to keep her here, she wishes to leave. We must find a truce.

Fortunately, I know of three other Omegas like Rose. Each one a *Hew-man*, or human. Each one mated to a king.

I call the Wanderer King first. Khan was like me, preferring to let his councilors do the bulk of the ruling while he wandered the galaxies, looking for Omegas; for a queen. Word is he's home more now that he has one.

The orb pulses with a purple glow before going dark. Khan declined my call.

No use calling the Hunter King, not if I want information. That only leaves King Aurus—the most talkative Alpha I know. He loves the sound of his own voice.

He'll answer my call, if only to gloat about his gaudy gold castle and golden-haired Omega.

Sure enough, the magical orb pulses only a few times before Aurus's face appears.

"Learned King," he hails me with a grin.

"That is what they called my father."

Most of the time, I don't allow others to see me through the orbs. But today, in the spirit of sharing information, I allow my visage to be seen, along with a view of my desk and walls of ancient scrolls behind me. *Learned King* indeed.

"I was being polite," Aurus says. "Bestian. Beast King. What is that on your face?"

"A mask."

"The Stone King really did his best to eradicate your lineage with that curse," Aurus says with his usual lack of tact. "How disfigured are you?"

"That's none of your concern. I'm alive, despite the evil one's best efforts."

Aurus lounges back in his giant golden throne. "So I can see. How can I help you?"

"I seek knowledge of humans."

"*Hoo-mans?* Why? Looking to get your hands on an Earth-born Omega?"

So that's what her planet is called. I file that tidbit away. I do not want to reveal much about my Rose, but Aurus's gloating is too much. "Maybe I already have."

He snaps out of his slouch. "You have an Omega? Congratulations. Join the club."

"Club?"

"It's an expression my Kim taught me. You will find your Omega takes over your life. Turns it upside down. Changes it."

I remain silent.

"Still in denial? The relationship must be new. How did you find her, anyway? My magicians have had no luck finding the lost *Hoo-man* Omegas."

"Lost Omegas? How many?"

Aurus shrugs. "No one knows. We found the lab where they worked to import them from Earth, but all records were destroyed. Apparently, the Stone King—your dead buddy—learned that we had acquired the Ogsul technology and serum necessary to import *Hoo-man* females and turn them into Omegas. When he heard that I ordered my magicians to find me an Omega of my own, he bribed some of them to work for him, instead."

"Bribed?" My disbelief is evident in my tone. "The Stone King?"

Aurus waves his hand. "Or he threatened them, compelled them... whatever. In any case, he got them to replicate the process and bring over more *Hoo-man* females. The Omegas were supposed to be delivered to the Stone Kingdom, but the deal must have gone bad, as my Kim would say. It seems the magicians panicked and fled before they could complete their task. As a result, the *Hoo-man* Omegas were scattered all over. One turned up in Arboron. Now, it seems, one ended up in your palace."

"Nearby." For the millionth time, I thank Ulf Rose wasn't found by an Alpha soldier first. My little moonflower might have been claimed by another. The thought makes me clench my fists, my claws pricking my palms. "I need all records regarding the human Omegas," I tell Aurus. "Anything your magicians have observed—all readings of the human vital signs, the serum effects, everything." I need to know if my mate is healthy.

"I'll send them, if you agree to share any findings with me," Aurus says. It's unlike him to be so forthcoming, but this is a special circumstance. His concern for his queen overcomes any posturing he would normally indulge in.

"Agreed. And if there is any information on successful Ulfarri-human offspring outcomes, I need that too."

"Is she pregnant already?" Aurus smiles again. Not his usual punchable grin, but something softer. "I do not have any of that, not yet. But Khan does, and he's already shared it with my magicians. We must do all we can to care for our Omegas."

I raise my chin in agreement.

"You should be called the Learned King, as your father was," Aurus says. "You are as scholarly as any Beta magician. You studied medicine, as well?"

His words are a dagger in my heart, but I keep the pain off my face. "Yes, as part of my extensive studies. My father insisted."

"I remember. You were seeking a cure to the curse that befell your kingdom. You found it."

"I was too late." I lie by telling the truth.

Aurus doesn't know the whole truth. No one does. I found a potion to heal the curse, but not cure it. The only cure was my father's sacrifice. And it killed both him and my mother.

"Was that before the..." Aurus circles his face with his finger.

"The potion the Stone King sent to *help*, which turned out to be poison that disfigured me?" If Aurus isn't going to be tactful, then neither am I. "It was during." The lowest point of my life. Medela was cursed, my mother was ill, everyone was dying. In the final stages of the curse, the sickness turned the sufferer to stone. I was desperate to find the cure—so desperate that I did as I am doing now, and scoured the far kingdoms for help. Kings and magicians from all over Ulfaria sent us potential remedies. Including the Stone King.

I later came to learn that the Stone King had in fact created the curse—the Red Death—as well. He was jealous of my father, and coveted my Omega mother. I have no proof and now that the evil bastard is dead, I never will. But all evidence points to him as the creator of both the curse, and the poison that ravaged my face.

Aurus presses his lips together. I prefer his silence to his prying. I would cut the connection between us, but I need to cultivate his good will.

I'm saved from the awkward pause in the conversation by a female voice calling, "Honey, I'm home!" I tense, and swivel to check on my sleeping Rose. The new voice at Aurus's back sounds so much like my own mate. That can only mean—

Aurus's whole face softens. In the distance, outside of the orb's displayed image, a door slams. And then—

The Golden King's eyes widen. There's a shrieking whistle. Aurus roars and throws up his arms before his entire person—and ridiculously gaudy throne—disappear in a burst of smoke.

Off-screen, someone is cackling. The newcomer strides into view. A tiny, pale-skinned human with spiky yellow hair, she saunters through a cloud of gray smoke with a large black gun cocked on one shoulder. Ulfarri troops call the guns *Chitin-Killers*. This one looks modified somehow, but is still almost bigger than the petite Omega.

"Kim!" Aurus shouts from somewhere off-screen. "What have I told you about shooting rocket launchers in the throne room?"

"You said it was outlawed by the king's royal decree. But you shoot off in the throne room all the time. Fair's fair. Besides," she pats the gun, "this isn't a rocket launcher. It's a

Chitin-Killer. Terral and his engi-nerd buddies designed it for me, for the next time I go into battle."

"We have discussed this." Aurus sounds exasperated. "You will absolutely not be going into battle—"

"Ah, ah!" Kim tips the gun to point it in the direction of his voice. "You say no but I say yes, and I'm holding the modified *Chitin-Killer*. It won't kill you—we replaced the rockets with smoke bombs—but it'll hurt." The little human stalks to the throne, which has tipped onto its side, and leans against it. "Besides, you promised not to talk to anyone about humans or Omegas without me."

"How did you know I was speaking about *Hoo-mans*?" Aurus says.

"I programmed an alarm to warn me if you say the word *Hoo-man* to any of your video-phone magic orb thingies."

"For the love of Ulf..." Aurus grumbles something about it being a mistake to let an Omega talk to a magician. I have never heard the Golden King sound so flustered. It is wonderful, and I am relishing every second.

Kim swings around and squints at me through the orb. "Hello. I'm Kim, from Earth. Who are you, and why were you talking about human Omegas? Do you have one?"

It would be in my best interest not to answer but once again I can't help myself. "Greetings, Kim. I am the King of Medela, and yes, I have procured an Omega."

Kim glares at me. The amount of fury emanating out of such a tiny body is impressive. "I'm sure she loves how you make it sound like you picked her out of a SkyMall magazine. How did you *procure* her? In a space station? At an auction?"

"Neither. She kicked down the door to my castle, broke a decades' old spell, and brought me to life."

Kim's head jerks back a beat. "Damn, that's pretty badass. Kinda like a reverse Sleeping Beauty."

All this time, Aurus has been creeping up behind the toppled throne, attempting a sneak attack on his tiny queen. Without looking back, Kim adjusts the gun to point over her shoulder. "I wouldn't, Gold-Daddy."

Aurus halts mid-step. "You will cease referring to me as your father."

"You don't like that? A little kink and role-play can increase sperm count. I read that in a magazine in my dentist's waiting room, and magazines in dentists' waiting rooms never lie." She winks at him and turns back to me.

"Listen, Mr. Masked Singer, if you've really got your hands on a human, I need to talk to her ASAP. Me, and possibly Emma and Haley. She'll be feeling like she's all alone in the world, and needs someone to talk to. Did she have a family back on Earth?"

"She says she did not." She also told me she considered the one she calls *Ma*, the healer she was living with, to be her new family. Her new home. And I am refusing to let her return. Since when have I become so heartless?

"Well, that doesn't mean she's not homesick. Talking to us will help."

Aurus's little Omega is wise as well as fearless. "I will consider it."

"Do that." Kim fixes me with a dead-eye stare, and points the gun in my direction. "But don't take too long. Otherwise, I'll come find her myself, and—*oof!*"

With Kim's gun pointed at me through the orb, Aurus is able to pounce. He grabs her and they both tumble out of sight. The gun goes flying. There's more chuckling and growling off-screen.

"You will pay for that, Omega." Aurus's husky threat drifts up to me. He sounds so content, I could retch. I can almost smell his Alpha pheromones through the orb.

"Pu-lease," Kim sounds breathless, "getting shot probably increases sperm count, too—"

I wave a hand, and the orb goes black. Not a moment too soon. At the last Kings' Council, Aurus smugly informed us that he was going to breed his Omega. Now that I have met his Kim, I doubt the Golden King has any control over her.

These human Omegas are not what they seem. They are brave and wily and have more power over us than we realize.

That's something to think about. But I must think fast, because when I check the orb for the nesting room, I find my Rose is awake and, once again, she's trying to leave.

THIRTEEN

Rose

This morning when I wake, I don't linger. I grab a sweet cake and stuff it in my mouth. After a quick stop in the bathroom, I rush down the hall to the balcony Rogue led me to last night.

When I get to the doors, I can see a bolt has been slid into place across them, locking them. I reach out to shift it but my hand never makes it to the surface. Something invisible cushions it, stopping me from touching it.

Bestian said he had conjured a magical barrier around the perimeter of the castle. Maybe he put one around the palace now, too.

The hem of my dress flares. Rogue has found me. It flows around my ankles, playing with my boot laces.

"Good morning," I say. "Can you show me another door?"

The little wind obeys, tugging my hem forward. But every door or window it leads me to is locked, and the same forcefield prevents me from unlocking or smashing through them. I pick a random window and try to break it using throw pillows, a vase, my left boot, and a chair. Each item bounces off—but slowly, like the forcefield is syrupy and wants to let each item down gently.

"Damn him." I tug my boot back on and tie the laces. I can't get out of the palace. Not this way. But this place is huge. There's got to be some exit Bestian forgot to block. A fire escape or something. Isn't barring all exits a fire hazard? Or maybe the doors will open in the event of an emergency.

It's more likely the wind servants will douse any fire, fix any problem, before it can cause damage.

That reminds me—Bestian promised he'd send *whisps* to check on Ma.

"Have you seen Ma?" I ask Rogue. I get silence, which I take to be a no. "Did one of your wind friends see her?"

The *whisp* blows in a circle around me. I'll take that as a yes. "Was she all right? Did she need anything?" Two questions, but Rogue blows harder. A nearby blanket flies off the settee it was strewn over, and settles around my shoulders.

The little wind is trying to comfort me. "I'm okay," I tell it. "I want to see her. Can you help me?"

Rogue goes silent. I'm about to accept that answer as a negative when it flurries around my legs and zooms down the hall, making curtains flare in its wake. I scurry after it.

It leads me to a long gallery hung with portraits. On the left side, the wall is broken up by a small alcove lit by glow orbs. The wind tugs me towards one.

"What is this?" There's a bench hugging the walls of the alcove. As I stand there, Rogue brings one of the orbs out to hover in front of me. The thing looks like a witch's gazing ball, with stormy gray tendrils of fog writhing over its smooth surface. I reach out to touch it, but a forcefield repels my hand, just like the one barring all exits. It has to be some kind of spell.

"I'm not sure what—" I begin, then the image on the

ball's surface changes. Ma's cottage appears in the mist, the picture coming into focus. There's Ma, digging in her garden, and Leelah is standing beside her.

"Any word from Rose?" Leelah's voice comes through clearly but sounds as if she's far away.

"Not yet. The king sent word that she was safe. Plus a formal notice that she is the king's choice in the Queen Covenant. There will be an announcement soon."

"That's wonderful!" Leelah claps her hands. "Who would have thought your Rose would be chosen? Such a great honor."

Ma glowers at her, then glances at the cottage gate. There's a cluster of Alpha soldiers just beyond the wall. Are they guarding Ma? Or imprisoning her?

"Perhaps," Ma says. "I'll celebrate after I've spoken to Rose. The king didn't mention whether he'll allow her to visit, but knowing my Rose, she won't take kindly to being told what to do."

I open my mouth but Ma can't see or hear me. It's like watching a movie. Or security cam footage.

I turn away from the orb. "Okay. I've seen enough." If I can't escape soon, maybe I can figure out a way to send word to Ma. "Thank you," I tell Rogue. "Will you show me the rest of the castle?"

The *whisp* whips around my neck so fast, it tickles. Despite myself, I giggle.

I follow Rogue down the gallery. When I pause to take in the pictures, I gasp. The elements in them are actually moving. Leaves on trees flutter in invisible breezes, lake surfaces ripple, and clouds float across painted skies. I hurry to check the portraits of actual people, kind of relieved to see how still they are. So it's just the landscapes which move. Curiouser and curiouser.

A newer-looking painting dominates the far wall at the

end, commanding my attention. I move closer to inspect it. A kind-eyed female gazes out from the canvas. She's wearing a crown. So is her much larger, emerald-skinned partner. An Omega queen and her Alpha king. They're standing outside in a bower of moonflowers. The tiny petals, the couple's eyes, the suns above their heads—they're not moving, but they all seem to glow. The whole thing is so realistic, I wouldn't be surprised if the figures took a breath and stepped out from the canvas.

"I see you found my parents." Bestian's voice echoes down the gallery. Tingles rise on the back of my neck. I quiver, hungering for his warmth, his scent.

I suck in a breath through my mouth, denying myself so I can hold onto my senses for as long as possible.

But when I turn, the sight of him hits me. His body looms, enormous in the huge space. Back home, he'd be a giant, a superhero with teal skin and striking tattoos. Everything about him—his size, his voice, his presence—proclaims him as Alpha.

He's irresistible. Damn him.

He comes closer, stepping out of the shadows and into the light. He's wearing a cloak but the hood is down. I gaze at him greedily. A mask covers the top half of his face, molded to his cheekbones and going down one side of his jaw. What it reveals is absolutely gorgeous. The structure of his face takes my breath away.

The mask matches the deep teal of his skin. His markings are a shimmering emerald green—just like his eyes. He does have the sexiest eyes. His hair, brows, and lashes are the deep, glossy blue of the ocean.

"Good morning," he greets me. My captor has good manners. Between that and his stunning looks, it takes me a moment to remember that I'm mad at him.

I summon my inner New Yorker, sharp accent and all.

"It was a good morning, until I found out I couldn't leave. I'm surprised you didn't lock me in my room."

He regards me calmly. "There was no need."

"Because you barricaded the palace."

"I could not be sure the magical border around my castle would hold you. So you're confined inside. For now."

He's so fucking sexy. It's not fair. I turn my back on him. It hurts to be this close to him and not in his arms. I want to be strong, but resisting him is so fucking hard.

"It needn't be like this, little one." He comes closer. There's a slight purr in his voice.

I hold up a hand, ignoring the warmth that rushes through my belly. "Don't. Did you send word to Ma?"

"You know I did. I instructed my *whisp* to show you proof, if you desired."

So that's why Rogue allowed me to see the orb. It was following orders.

"However, I did not instruct it to show you the gallery. It seems this particular *whisp* has a sense of loyalty towards you, rather than to me, its master." Bestian sounds stern.

Right now, said *whisp* is cowering at my feet.

I whirl to face the king. "Please don't hurt Rogue. It's only trying to help me."

"You named the *whisp*?" He sounds incredulous.

I close the distance between us and reach out to touch him. My hand looks so tiny on his corded, muscular forearm. "Please, Bestian." I couldn't bear it if he ordered the little *whisp* to go and never return. "Rogue is my only friend."

"I am your friend," he informs me.

I swallow and retract my hand. "I still don't trust you. I barely know you." *And for some reason, you seem hell-bent on keeping me here when I've made it clear I want to leave.*

He pins me with his gaze but after a moment, his

shoulders soften. "Then you should have an ally. The *whisp* may stay by your side. But only if it abides by my will, as well."

"Thank you." Rogue twirls gently around my boots, then I can't feel it anymore. I remain where I am, gazing up at Bestian. "You're wearing a mask."

He cocks his head. "My own creation. Do you like it?"

"Yes." I want to deny it, but from the way it hugs his features, I can tell he has the bone-structure of a god. I still want to see his face, but he's so damn sensitive about it. "It suits you."

He shifts back a step and offers his arm to me. "Will you walk with me?"

I pause for a moment, considering. He didn't demand. He didn't just sweep me up into his arms like a doll. He asked. I have right of refusal. And now that I know Ma isn't worried sick about me...

Let us come to an accord, he said last night.

Maybe I can't escape right away. Maybe the king and I are at war, and with his superior strength and knowledge, he will win. But he wants my agreement, my acceptance.

Maybe I can negotiate with him.

Maybe I'm here for a reason.

"A truce," I agree, and put my hand on his arm.

FOURTEEN

Rose

"I want to speak to Ma," I tell Bestian as he leads me through the dazzling palace.

"That can be arranged."

"Really? You'll let me—"

"You won't be leaving the castle, but you can still talk to her. Is this acceptable?"

"Yes." *For now.*

He walks me down a staircase and into a long corridor. The air is cooler here, and it smells like books.

The first door opens to reveal a cozy room with a huge table covered in sheets of parchment. A massive chair hugs the table, facing the door. Behind it there's a wall with rows and rows of cubby holes, each one holding a scroll.

"What is this place?"

"My study. You would have found it eventually on your wanderings." Bestian leads me towards the table. As we pass, rounded stones inset into the walls on both sides of us flare to life. The stones glow orange and dark purple, giving off warmth like heat lamps set into a vertical fireplace of some sort. "If ever the door is warded, I'm conducting an experiment and you are not to attempt to enter. My warding spells do not always work on you, and my experiments can be dangerous." The muscles of his teal arm are tense, as if he expects me to disagree.

"That's fair. Safety first."

"Yes. Your safety above all."

A trio of large orbs is suspended above the desk, each one glowing blue.

"Those orbs." I point. "Do you use them to spy on people?"

He waves a hand and the center one rotates. There, on the rounded screen, is a familiar bed and pile of pillows— the room where I've been sleeping.

I press my lips together. "So you've been watching me."

"Of course. I find you endlessly fascinating." There's a chuckle lurking behind his amused tone.

"Your life is very boring and sad."

"Or you, above all beings in the known universe and beyond, are the one most worthy of study. I will spend the rest of my life learning you."

Awww, flattery. I'd brush it off, but my cheeks are glowing as hot as the fireplace stones. Something about his voice, his scent, his eyes intent on my face... my heart flutters despite myself. I used to long for a guy to speak to me this way. I bought all the lies my past boyfriends told me —right up to the point where they each broke my heart.

But Bestian isn't lying. He means every sappy word. And that scares me most of all.

He guides me to sit in the huge chair. I perch on the seat. With my feet dangling a few inches off the ground, I feel like Goldilocks trespassing too far.

"I promised you could talk to Matron. And so you shall."

"All right."

"My *whisps* have made ready." He rests one giant hand on my shoulder and waves another at the central orb. The image of my room disappears, replaced by the familiar, comforting sight of Ma's fireplace and chair. My throat tightens. I lean forward. Bestian doesn't hold me back, but his hand slides to the back of my neck, collaring it loosely. My pulse thrums under his fingers.

"Ma?" I call. Her tall, elegant form glides into sight.

"Rose?" Her eyes light up and she breaks into a smile.

"Ma, it's me." Even though I just spied on her, it's good to see her face. Her mauve skin is unmarred, her blue eyes no longer sunken and tired. "You look well."

"As do you, my dear."

My shoulders soften. It really is her. "How are you feeling?"

"Much better, thanks to the king." She squints at me, and I know she's noticing the king's hand at the back of my neck. Bestian's standing beside me, mostly out of her line of vision, but his presence can't be denied.

"I didn't make it to the river in time," I tell her. "The Alphas found me. I ran—and the king... rescued me." *Out of the frying pan...*

"I see." Ma looks calm, but she's studying me closely.

"I don't know how it happened," I lie. I'm not going to mention the illegal potion she's been giving me, not with the king right here. "Something triggered my estrus. Apparently, I'm actually an Omega. A human one. Who knew?" I force out a chuckle.

"Oh Rose," Ma murmurs.

"I'm all right," I rush. "This palace is lit. And I get all the sweet cakes I could ever want."

"The king treats you well?"

A purr erupts behind me. The tension in my back melts away and my whole body sinks into the seat.

"Very well." I try to fight it, but a dreamy quality enters my voice. "Like a queen."

Bestian clears his throat. The orb rises and floats backwards to display both me in the chair and the Alpha beside it.

"Your Majesty." Ma bows her head.

"Matron Marphel. You found and cared for the king's Omega. You are to be commended."

Ma says nothing, but her lips purse.

"As a token of my gratitude, allow my wind servants to remain by your side. Nothing will replace Rose, but the *whisps* can help you."

"I'm honored, Your Majesty." Ma's voice is tart. There's a lot she's not saying.

I blink, but between the effect of the purr and the heat rising in my core, my thoughts are swimming backwards.

"Say goodbye, my little moonflower," Bestian orders.

"Goodbye, Ma. I'll see you soon," I add.

The orb dims and Ma disappears. I lean back in the chair, too relaxed to care. I want to turn and rub myself against Bestian. His purr always calms me, but why am I now getting excited as well? A tingling warmth is spreading through my chest and belly.

"Thank you," I manage. I don't ask when I can speak to Ma again. Even if he says no, I'll find a way to see her. The *whisps* will help me.

My thoughts feel very far away.

"It appears you are going into heat again, Omega." Bestian's purr increases in volume. The sound vibrates through my body. Goosebumps prickle over my skin and I clench my thighs. "And have no fear—I will rut you very, very soon. But first, I have one more thing to show you."

My little moonflower's eyes are dark, glittering pools, signaling the onset of estrus. Her sweet, musky perfume rises in a cloud. My cock strains in my breeches as I guide her further down the hall with a heavy hand on her slender back. My purr is deepening, roughening, turning almost into a growl.

When Rose spoke to the healer who took her in, I sensed her tension. My purr was automatic; I had not anticipated its effect on her. The ancient scrolls describe how an Alpha's scent, voice, and protective behavior can trigger an Omega's heat. But Rose is not a typical Omega. We cannot know whether her estrus follows normal patterns.

Still, here is proof that she is attuned to me. She might deny it, but her body knows the truth.

Her willowy form sways ahead of me. At the end of the long corridor, the *whisps* pull open the doors.

Rose's steps falter. "Where are you taking me?"

"You will see. It's a surprise. I believe you will like it."

She turns her head and blinks at me. "I've never felt like this before. With anyone. I didn't think it was possible."

"It is partly the Omega in you. But that you react so strongly to *me* just proves that Ulf intended you for me. You were meant to find me. You were meant to be mine."

"That's ridiculous," she mutters. "All that soulmate bullshit—people say that back home, and it's not true."

"You don't believe in soul-bonded mates?"

She screws her face up, struggling to answer. I find it adorable that she's determined to fight me, even in her blissful state. "If that's the same thing as soulmates, then yes. It's a lie to sell sappy greeting cards and perpetuate the myth of the perfect nuclear family."

"Then why are you so drawn to me?"

"There has to be a practical explanation." She cocks her head. "The purr. It does something to me."

The rumble in my chest increases in volume. "It affects you. As you affect me. No, don't argue. Relax and let yourself be."

She sighs.

"I will not leave you wanting long, little one. But first, your gift."

I urge her forward. She's half walking, half leaning back against me by the time we reach the doors. The rich moonflower fragrance hits my nose first, along with the sound of running water.

"What..." Her head falls back against my chest, her mouth open. The giant space before us is bigger than any ballroom. Two sets of stairs curve away from the doors, leading to a crystalline lake. A waterfall crashes from an invisible platform into one side of the pool. Glowing moonflower vines grow in lush groves around the water. Above our heads, the ceiling stretches in a vast black expanse, deep as an endless pool, dark as the midnight sky. Tiny lights twinkle everywhere like jewels.

Rose stares, drinking in the sight. "How is this possible?"

"Magic," I whisper. The *whisps* race around the room, stirring the vines. A few tendrils climb to reach us, bursting into bloom at our feet.

"It's a garden... inside the palace."

"My mother spent most of her time here. She cultivated the moonflowers." I pluck a tiny, purple-toned one from a nearby vine and tuck it behind her ear.

"It's forbidden to pick the moonflowers," Rose says.

"For all but the king. Or queen," I add.

Her mouth snaps shut.

I wait a few moments while she looks her fill. "Do you like it?"

"It's beautiful," she admits.

"It's yours. And there's more." I usher her onto a platform and call the *whisps* to carry us past the waterfall. There, in a secret grotto, is the queen's study. It's much like mine, with a large work table and chair, and heatstones built into the wall. A fire in the corner roars to life as we enter.

Living moss and hanging plants are woven into the walls. Rose pauses to absorb it all, her fingertips hovering inches away from the dark green leaves. "There must be specimens of every type of Ulfarri flora here," she breathes.

I chuckle. "Not every type, but many. More importantly, this library holds mountains of rare knowledge and treatises on Omegas." I wave a hand at the scrolls and books arranged neatly on their shelves. "I have borrowed some of them for my own study. The rest are here. I can teach you what I know of Omegas, but you might want to learn more on your own."

"I can't read Ulfarri."

I frown. "You have a translator chip."

"It doesn't work on the written word."

The Beta magicians who pulled the humans through the portal must have turned off some of the translator chips' functions. Whoever ordered these Omegas must not have wanted them to read. "The chip should have visual functionality," I say. "With your permission, I will have the *whisps* examine it while you sleep. If there is a simple way to modify it so you can read, they can do that." The silence stretches between us until I offer, "Or, if you prefer, I can simply teach you to read our language."

Her eyelashes flutter. Her scent mingles sweetly with

the pervasive fragrance from the moonflowers. I can't tell what she's thinking. "You would do that?"

"It would be my honor."

"Tell the *whisps* they can examine the chip. If they can't get it to work, then you can teach me." She offers me a small smile. "I'd like to know more about being an Omega."

I step close. I'm going deeper into rut, and can't keep myself from touching her any longer. My hand goes to the back of her neck, kneading lightly. "In the meantime, I can tell you what I know." My voice is gruff.

"All right," she says.

"When an Omega goes into estrus, it can last for days. Weeks, even. Then it will fade for a time before returning—"

"Kind of like a period," Rose interrupts me. "Humans have something similar," she adds. "But not nearly as intense as this... thank god. Anyway, sorry. Please continue."

"Thank you. As I was saying, the estrus cycles continue for the duration of an Omega's fertile years, only stopping when she is successfully bred and gestating."

"You mean pregnant?"

"Yes. But all our knowledge was collated before the birth rates dropped—not to mention, only Ulfarri Omegas were studied. There's a good chance human Omegas—or those created by the serum—are different. It's highly unlikely you'd already be pregnant after your first estrus."

"Okay." She sounds drowsy. I pull her into my arms before she sways to the floor. She's so small. Even with her curls loose and swaying in a halo around her head, the tips don't reach my chin.

"But it is possible for a human Omega to be bonded with an Alpha, and bear his offspring." My heart pounds with excitement at the mere thought. "My darling little moonflower, I cannot wait to breed you."

A tremor runs through her. Fear? Anticipation? Her scent thickens the air around us. My cock is throbbing—an insistent, dull ache. Leaning down, I rub my cheek over the top of her head, basking in her perfume.

"The nesting is a good sign," I whisper into her ear.

"I should be freaking out right now. But I'm too relaxed. What does bonded mean?"

"A bond forms between an Omega and her Alpha mate when he claims her. The studies I saw were unclear about when exactly the bond forms—it can be a gradual process, or happen instantly, especially in a soul-bond—but most agree that the advent is the claiming bite."

"Claiming bite?"

"Yes." I trace the delicate skin of her neck. She shivers again. "As you know, an Alpha is not immune to an Omega's scent when she's in the throes of estrus. He responds to her by going into rut—the Alpha version of estrus. His first priority is to take his Omega—to rut her."

"Mmm," Rose murmurs dreamily.

"His next instinct is to claim her fully by biting her. To mark her as his, imbue her with his scent, to ward off competition. He can bite her anywhere on her body, and they will be bound for life." I can't prevent my voice from thickening as I describe it. There is no doubt that I want to claim my little moonflower, and that desire grows stronger every day. I came so close the other night...

"Does it hurt?"

"It can. But it seems Omegas are wired to enjoy the pain. In fact, some have described it as the ultimate ecstasy."

"I don't know. It sounds pretty intense. Not to mention permanent."

"It is both of those things."

"Do you want to... claim me?" Her voice is soft, hesitant.

With everything inside of me. But something keeps holding me back. I reach for an evasive answer. "As an Alpha, I have that instinct, of course. Do you want me to?" I hold my breath as I await her reply.

She swallows. "I don't know. Permanent sounds so... permanent."

Her words are like needles in my heart but I keep my tone light. "Then we will wait until you are ready. No—until you *beg* me for it. And I promise you this: one day, you will beg for it, little one."

FIFTEEN

Rose

Two things I'm learning about Bestian—one: when it comes to knowledge about Omegas, he's a nerd. And two: when it comes to touching me, he's a god.

Truth be told, I'm pretty close to begging already.

His strong fingers massage the back of my neck as he tells me, "I've read that the bite creates such a strong bond between mates that they can sense each other's emotions. Fear. Pain. Happiness. Even when they're apart."

"How is that possible?"

"Magic."

"Of course." I don't care what he's saying, as long as he doesn't stop touching me. "I'm human," I remind him.

"The human Omegas on Ulfaria have bonded with their Alphas. Or so I've heard."

"Which reminds me... do you think I could meet them? Or one of them, at least?" I've been so distracted by everything that I kept forgetting to ask Bestian, but the chance to talk to someone else in my exact position—who knows exactly what I'm going through—would be unreal.

"I'm sure that can be arranged. In fact, one of them has already asked after you."

"What? When? Who?" Outraged that he didn't tell me this before, I huff out a breath and spin around to glare at him.

"Settle, little one." Reaching out, Bestian threads his claws into my hair and tugs my head back carefully so I'm drowning in the ocean depths of his gaze. "I simply forgot to mention it before now. My apologies."

Goddamn it, why can I never stay mad at him? Why is my tummy twisting with longing just from the way he's looking at me?

"It was Kim," he continues. "The Golden King's queen. Quite a handful, apparently, but she is wise, and brave."

To my astonishment, an acid flare of jealousy burns through my gut at his praise of another woman. Is this an Omega thing too? I don't remember being the rabidly jealous type. "Is she now?" I'm unable to hide my icy tone.

Bestian chuckles. "There it is, the famous Omega jealousy. There's no need to worry, my little moonflower. I only have eyes for you. You are smart, witty, and so very beautiful. The most perfect Omega of them all."

Infuriatingly, his words immediately ease my anxiety. I look away, my face hot. I've always loathed it when men put other women down to reassure their partners. And now here I am, lapping this shit up. The fuck is wrong with me?

"Do you deny it?"

"You're biased. And a nerd."

"Nerd?"

His confused tone brings my gaze back to his face. "Never mind. It's an Earth thing. But you are one. Believe me." My hand reaches of its own volition to touch his cheek through the mask. I want to see more of him.

"It is not to be," he says, and I realize I spoke aloud. He takes my questing hand in his giant one.

"I want to touch you," I whisper. The drowsy intoxication I felt earlier has faded, replaced by new waves of tingling heat in my lower belly.

"Then touch me, little Omega." He slashes the front of his shirt with a claw and the fabric peels away from his muscular chest. My palms ache to feel his gleaming skin.

There's an argument I'm supposed to be making but it's slipping away. My clit is thrumming insistently, distracting me. "I'm not an Omega," I mumble.

His sudden growl makes me jump. A little moan escapes me, and my pussy flutters deliciously.

"Do you need proof?" His eyes—glittering dark pools in the gloom—have me frozen in place. He retracts his claws and then, while one arm clamps around me, his other hand delves under my dress. His finger finds my nether lips, sliding between them to release a gush of my juice, and the groan that comes out of me doesn't sound human. It's raw. Primal. Desperate. He finds my throbbing bud and circles it for a tantalizing moment before bringing his dripping fingertip up to waggle it in the air between us.

Need crashes through me.

"You are an Omega, Rose. Only an Omega would respond to me this way. Only an Omega produces this kind of slick." As if to prove his point, he licks it off his finger, his eyes never leaving mine.

I can only stare at him, as if he's hypnotized me. The ache in my sex is excruciating.

"You may not be Ulfarri, but I don't care. And I don't care where you came from. Ulf saw fit to reach across the universe and bring you to me." His eyes flash. "Now, you are mine. And mine you will stay."

My heart is pounding and there's a twist in my lower belly at his words. Fear? Lust? I can't tell.

Bestian looms over me. "No more fighting it. You will submit to your true nature." I can't move—I'm imprisoned by his iron-hard arm. "You will submit to me."

He growls again and my whole body convulses. I close my eyes as white hot stars burst behind my eyelids. My legs give out but Bestian scoops me up. On sheer instinct, I lock my legs around him and rock my hips forward, seeking maximum contact.

"So eager, little Omega."

A pained sound escapes my throat. I strain closer, frantic to relieve the pounding need in my core.

"Easy," he soothes. His huge hands find my ass, cupping and lifting me. He's holding me up as I grind my aching, throbbing clit against him. Tiny climaxes sparkle and fizzle between my thighs, building to a crescendo.

"Bestian!"

"Yes, little one, say my name. Your body knows what it was made for, even if you deny it."

The tension in my belly coils tighter.

"Bestian..." I'm panting. His green eyes are almost black with lust.

"Ask me for it. Tell me what you need.""

I'm too far gone to care that I'm begging. "Growl for me again. Please."

A rumbling earthquake erupts from his chest, shaking me to the core. It triggers an avalanche that pulls me under. I come with a ragged shout, shuddering in his arms.

I must have blacked out for a second, because when I come to, I'm blinking at the ceiling. Red firelight licks the shadows.

A monster is rearing over me. Bestian's hulking form is half in light, half in shadow. He's naked, his massive torso an imposing combination of tattooed muscles and a few pitted scars. He passes a hand over me and, with a few flicks of his claws, my clothing falls away.

"Omega," he purrs, squeezing my breasts until I gasp. He reaches down to cup my sex and I jack-knife up, reaching for him.

He leans back, pulling me to straddle his giant frame, stretching my legs wide. I slide down, seeking his cock. Even though I just came, there's a gnawing, unsatisfied ache in my pussy. I rock over the ridge of his pulsing shaft, whimpering when my clit catches it at just the right angle. I brace my hands on his broad shoulders, trying to impale myself on his thick length.

Bestian grips my hips, stilling me. "Patience."

"Now," I growl. My fingers arch and dig into his taut pecs. I would claw him if it would get him inside me faster.

His chuckle reverberates through me. He lifts me and his cock springs up, flinging drops of my own slick up to paint my belly. "Is this what you want?"

"Yes." I'm straining my thighs, trying to fight his hold and sink down onto him. My dripping pussy is just inches away from his cockhead. I could scream with frustration.

"Are you sure? You want to feel me deep inside your tight, pink, wet little cunt?"

"Yes! Please!"

"Do you think you can take it?" His mocking, calm tone is as infuriating as it is hot. "Can you handle my big, hard cock and even bigger, harder knot? Or do I need to make you come a few more times first? You're already dripping but—"

"No!" I howl. "I can handle it! Please fuck me! I promise I can take it!"

"Then take it." With ridiculous ease, he lines himself up and enters me slowly... inch by excruciating inch. He's so huge, stretching me so wide—the mere thought is enough for my pussy to clench hard, another spurt of juice easing his path.

"Do you see, Omega? Do you see how slick you get for me?" He scoops some up and feeds it to me. I suck his finger with greedy abandon. The scent makes my eyes roll back in my head.

He grips the back of my neck with a huge hand, forcing me to focus, then thrusts hard, forcing the rest of his cock in to the hilt. I close my eyes and gasp at the intense, painful pleasure of being filled so fully.

"Is this how a human responds to her puny male?"

A giggle escapes me. I can't help it. Not one of the arrogant models and executives I dated—with their Botoxed features and oiled muscles—could hold a candle to Bestian's powerful body and beautiful face. "No," I admit.

Bestian draws light, lazy circles over my clit until I cry out, then brings his wet finger to my lips. I flick my tongue against it, relishing the way my own flavor explodes on my tongue. He rakes the tips of his claws over my breasts, stopping to slap each one lightly. The pain sparks, shooting straight to my throbbing core.

"No. This is how you respond to me. Your Alpha. Your mate." He sounds so smug, so self-assured but I can't argue. I don't want to.

He's deep inside me, stretching me wide, just where I want him—but he's not moving, and my strained thighs won't co-operate when I try to ride him. So I swivel my hips, whimpering, willing him to give me everything I crave.

He massages my neck, supporting me as I arch my back, trying to fit more of him inside of me. My insides are fluttering around his huge girth.

"Surrender," Bestian murmurs, and I've had enough of his torment.

"Shut up," I tell him. "Shut up and fuck me."

His abs stand out in stark relief as he tenses and sits up, leaning over so his glaring eyes are level with mine.

I lick my lips, the combination of fear and desire making my head spin as he places his huge hands on my waist, squeezing just hard enough to make me gasp.

He snaps his hips upwards, bouncing me on his cock. The movement drives him even deeper inside me. Bolts of pleasure explode through my core, fireworks that grow in size and intensity.

Bestian grips my waist harder, holding me in place while he hammers me from below. I'm on top, but he's definitely the one in control.

He slaps my breast, lightly but hard enough to sting. I shudder and clench around him.

"You like that, don't you, little one?" he growls, slapping me again. "I can feel your cunt squeezing my cock every time I hurt you, so there's no point in denying it."

He gives another hard thrust and I whimper as the pleasure builds... and builds... The bulge at the base of his cock—his knot—is growing, stretching me to the point of pain. Welding me to him.

"You're close, aren't you?" Bestian croons. "Are you going to be a good little girl and come all over my cock?"

He shifts his hips slightly, changing the angle of penetration, hitting a spot deep inside me which makes my thighs tremble.

"I'm aching to fill you up, little Omega." Bestian's voice reverberates through my very soul. All I can do is straddle him and take every fierce, precise thrust. "To shoot all my hot cum deep inside you... where it belongs. But first, you're going to come good and hard... so hard that your tight little cunt fucking *milks* me, for so long that you squeeze out every last drop—"

The sensations reach a crescendo and I snap. Waves of searing pleasure build deep inside my core and roll through my lower belly, my pussy rippling uncontrollably.

Bestian follows me over the edge with a roar, his knot pulsating in time with my contractions. I collapse against him, loose and limp as a blanket. I'm wrung out.

When his climax has subsided, Bestian leans back, taking me with him. He lets out a growl and yet more slick gushes from my battered and satisfied pussy, pooling between us. His fingers find my hair and tug my head back.

"That's my beautiful girl," he murmurs. I strain upwards to find his lips, kissing him with all the feelings I can't express. I taste myself on him. I taste him. And the blend of our essence is perfection.

SIXTEEN

Rose

I WAKE TO A DELICIOUS ACHE BETWEEN MY THIGHS. My inner muscles are stretched and sore. But I'm smiling. Hashtag no regrets.

Last night was incredible. I've never come from penetration only before. At least, I don't think I have. My memories of old lovers are faded and void of detail, but while I remember one or two of them being pretty good in bed, the rest left me with a palpable feeling of disappointment.

Last night blew all that away.

Rogue flutters over my face, stirring my hair. I'm back in the nesting room, lying on one side of the big bed. There's a big dent beside me, where Bestian slept. I don't remember him carrying me up here but the lingering heat tells me we cuddled all night.

My muscles protest as I sit up. Good thing Bestian isn't here; I need some time to recover.

The *whisp* carries an ornate sheet of parchment to my hand. My gaze drifts to the alien script: *My lovely Rose... I* grab it and gape at the calligraphy. I can read it. Bestian did what he promised—the *whisps* fixed my translator chip.

My lovely Rose,

Last night, we touched and held perfection. Let us set aside our differences and embrace what Ulf has given us.

Today, you will rest. The whisps will satisfy your every whim. Tonight, you will join me for dinner.

Commands and a compliment. I should toss the note across the room. Instead, I sniff the corners for lingering traces of Bestian's scent.

Fuck me, I'm into him.

The thought of leaving is getting less and less appealing. Yes, I want my freedom and the ability to visit Ma. But maybe there's a way I can have my sweet cakes and eat them, too.

Rogue teases the ends of my curls. I return Bestian's note and watch it float gently through the air.

"The king has informed me that I'm to join him for dinner," I tell the friendly *whisp* as I climb out of bed.

Rogue flurries past me, straightening the comforter and smoothing it over the corners of the bed.

"Don't worry, I'm planning to go. But I need your help."

The little wind weaves around my ankles like a cat.

Bestian wants a truce? He wants to *come to an accord?* I'll bargain with him until I hold all the cards. And then we'll see who truly rules.

I roll back my shoulders and give my first royal command. "Make me look like a queen."

This morning, I left Rose sleeping. I curse my royal duties, but the councilors who rule in Medea City in my stead are clamoring for my attention. They want advice about how to handle the Red Death.

I want nothing more than to remain with my Omega, but every time I think of her, the words she spoke to me in the beginning echo in my ear:

If you're the king, you should do something. Your people are dying.

I issue curt messages telling my advisors the Red Death is already being handled—that I distributed a potion that will reverse most symptoms. It's not a cure, but it is the culmination of the research I started when the curse first came upon the land. I send the bulk of my findings to my royal magicians, ordering them to continue to study the curse, track its spread, and appoint a committee to look after the afflicted.

"One more matter," another advisor says through a private channel. "I've heard rumors that you initiated the Queen Covenant and found an Omega."

I wave a hand, and my communication orbs go dark. I send the *whisps* with a final edict saying I am not to be disturbed.

My councilors know I initiated the Queen Covenant since they were the ones who received the royal decree the morning after Rose first appeared at my door. I was so desperate to find her that I had no choice but to go public with my search. However, they do not know what transpired after that, and I want to keep my Omega a secret—at least for now. It won't be possible forever, especially since Aurus now knows, but as selfish as it may seem, I want to keep her all to myself for as long as possible. I'm hoping news will take time to spread to Medela.

I tried to spy on Rose earlier, but the *whisp* informed me that she asked for privacy. I believe she was in the bathroom at the time. This is the first time she has not tried to leave immediately after waking up, and I can't describe how much that warms my heart.

She's plotting something. I can't wait to find out what it is. But there are hours between now and dinner time. I pray it is something good. She intrigues me, but she is troubled. No matter how close I get to her physically, I always sense some kind of invisible barrier between us. I can think of no other way to describe it.

I wonder if it has anything to do with the bad dreams she sometimes has.

I wander through the palace, checking the preparations being made by the *whisps*. Tonight must be perfect. I want to show my new mate all the pleasures of her new life.

When I reach the main ballroom where Rose first confronted me, my steps slow.

Perhaps I should issue an edict to offer aid to the afflicted. And a new committee to oversee research into the Red Death and any similar curses.

I look up. My pacing has brought me to the gallery, in front of my parents' portrait. My father looks wise and stern, my mother, loving and gentle.

"You would have loved her," I tell them. "Her wit, her beauty. Already, she has changed me."

A smile hovers over my mother's mouth. I would give anything to hear her voice again.

"Rose will make a great queen." She deserves a coronation. Then again, I never had one, deeming them unnecessary.

"Ruling is a burden and a privilege," my father told me

as I lay on my sick bed. *"When I am gone, you must take your place as king. Work every day to prove yourself worthy."*

But I haven't done that. The only thing I've done is found an Omega. And I didn't even find her—she found me.

A wave of shame fills my chest. The scars on my face itch and sting—a permanent reminder. Perhaps it is good my parents are long gone. It is a boon from Ulf, a relief, that they will never see the failure their son has become.

I turn away from my parents' portrait and force my thoughts in another direction. The day is waning and there is much to be done. Rose is making ready, and so will I. Tonight must be perfect. I will woo my Omega, and win her love.

Maybe then I will be worthy of a queen.

⁂

Rose

My dress is a wonder. I don't know how Rogue did it, but I am wearing something out of a Cinderella movie, except it's not sky blue, blush pink, or even moonflower red-black. It's all those colors and more, rippling like the sunset on the water, as astonishing as a glimpse of a galaxy. Piercing like the glare of a diamond, gleaming like the heart of a pearl. I might as well be wearing the whole of the night sky.

The last of the five moons is rising when I swish down the long portrait gallery towards the ballroom. My favorite *whisp* accompanies me, holding up my train. It also did something to secure my hair and the jewels it wove through my curls. Everything about this outfit is magic—or, if not magic, at least defying the laws of physics.

I pause under Bestian's parents' portrait, smoothing the front of my dress. Tonight feels like a first date.

"I guess it kind of is a first date," I tell Rogue. The low light from the glowing orbs catches on the painting, putting a glimmer in the queen's eye. She looks like she's gazing down at me.

"I won't break his heart," I tell her, and joke, "I'm not sure he has one." As soon as I say that, I know it's not true. He's finally stopped being quite so overbearing, and is trying to ease my path into my new life.

"He can be kind. But he's shut himself off from the world. I don't think that's the life you wanted for him."

The motionless queen has no answers for me, so I turn, leaving her and her Mona Lisa smile. The stretch of wall beyond the last king and queen's portrait is bare. There is no picture of Bestian.

My skirts rustle as I move down the long hall. The doors at the end swing open and I glide through them to find myself at the top of the staircase overlooking the ballroom, the one I entered when I first trespassed here.

The broken statues are gone. The room is illuminated by glowing orbs thronging every column. Overhead, the magical ceiling shimmers and froths with changing colors that match my dress.

Movement catches my eye and I look down. Bestian is waiting for me at the bottom of the stairs. My heart pounding, I smile at him. We're in the room where we first met, but we've swapped places. I wait for him to grin, to recognize the irony, but he just gazes up at me, looking stunned. He's staring at the top of my head.

I'm wearing a crown.

The weight of the silence between us is too heavy. I can't speak. Slowly, the huge Alpha ascends the stairs, stopping a few steps below the top when he's eye level with me.

"Bestian," I manage.

"Rose."

He's still gazing at me, but no longer at the crown. His gorgeous eyes are fixed on me. I had intended for him to acknowledge me as an equal, and he is. But I didn't anticipate what else I'd convey by wearing the crown.

At length, he climbs the rest of the steps. Now looming over me, he offers his arm and I take it. The spell wrought by his intense gaze is broken.

But as he ushers me onto a balcony where a table is set for two, I feel like I've crossed a line. I've forded the Rubicon, and there's no turning back now.

SEVENTEEN

Rose

"You look lovely," the king says, settling into his seat after pulling out my chair for me.

"So do you." Wow, I'm winning at conversation tonight. But Bestian does look incredible. He's in formal-looking robes that make him look kingly while doing nothing to obscure the breadth of his shoulders and back. His glossy black shirt is open at the neck, revealing enough to give me a glimpse of the powerful muscles of his chest.

I've been staring at him without speaking for too long. I lick my lips to make sure I'm not drooling.

"You changed your mask," I say. At first glance, the fabric looks black like his shirt, but every so often, it shimmers like the fabric of my dress.

"I asked my wind servants what you'd be wearing. They refused to tell me." He frowns, but I know him well enough to tell he's teasing. "It seems one naughty *whisp* spoils the whole bunch."

The wind around us stirs. Covered dishes float to the

table. "I made them keep it a secret," I admit. "I wanted to surprise you."

"You did." His gaze flicks up to my crown. I resist the urge to reach up and make sure it's in place.

Bestian's own head is bare but his thick blue hair is tied back in a ponytail, emphasizing his perfect cheekbones and strong, square jaw. I like him rough and shaggy, but it turns out he's just as hot when he's dressed up. "Do you have a crown?" I ask without thinking.

His gaze drops to the food the *whisps* are serving. It looks like some sort of stew, except it's purple. "Of course. Several. They're around here somewhere."

Of course he has crowns. He doesn't need to wear them around his own home, especially when there's no one else here. And when was the last time he even left the grounds?

A goblet that looks like it was carved from obsidian floats to my hand. I take it and sniff the amber liquid. "This is fancy."

"This is your life now." He sounds so smug, but weirdly, it doesn't make me bristle like it used to. Maybe I'm getting used to the idea. "You will dine with me every night."

I set the goblet down with a clink. "You mean, *Will you please dine with me tonight, Rose?*" I roll my eyes. "Didn't you ever learn how to court someone?"

"I never had to. I was a prince."

"And handsome." The *whisps* have made a centerpiece of glowing moonflowers on the table. The soft light caresses the fine planes of Bestian's jaw. The mask makes his emerald eyes look darker. Almost black.

"Once." Bestian's voice is tight. Ah yes, he's touchy about his looks.

"You should glance in a looking glass sometime. You're still hot. I bet you were a player."

"A player?"

"A guy who had many bed partners and no intention of committing to one." There's a little pang in my chest as I speak—like an echo of a past hurt. I choose to ignore it.

"An apt description of my former self. But I have no desire to speak of the past. Tell me, Rose, what you mean by *hot*."

"Handsome. Sexy. Appealing." I stop when I catch his amused expression.

"Go on," he drawls. "What about me is appealing?"

"Your face—what I can see of it. Your eyes. Your body." My skin tingles as I look him up and down. When I continue, my voice is huskier. "You're very... large."

"Do you like how large I am?"

I'm getting flustered, and take a sip of my drink to hide it. "You know I do. I've never come just from penetration before." Now, why did I choose to introduce that into the conversation? Cheeks burning, I drain half the contents of my goblet.

Bestian picks up his own glass and toasts me, smirking. I guess I can't begrudge him a smirk. He is a god in bed.

The *whisps* bring more delicious-smelling dishes of food to the table and I busy myself with filling my belly. For a while, there's nothing but the clink of our silverware and goblets. It's pleasant, eating across from Bestian like this. Domestic.

"This is nice. We've been almost civil," I tell him.

"Is it so hard to believe we could come to an accord?"

"I'd made up my mind to fight you," I admit.

"Why?"

It's a good question. He can fuck my brains out however and whenever he wants, but every time Bestian talks about *soulmates* or *forever*, something makes me want to run.

Something intangible; something I can't describe. "I like a challenge," I say at last, because it's true.

"You make a formidable opponent. But in the end, you will lose. This is your life now, Rose. You can fight me all you want—I enjoy it—but in the end, you will surrender."

I tap a fingernail against my goblet. He's right. Until now, I've surrendered every time. My body betrays me.

"You know you belong here. You look like a queen."

"According to you, I am one." I raise my chin. "Is that not the truth?"

He toasts me again. "I will give you anything you want, Rose."

"Except my freedom. A life outside the castle walls."

"Except for that," he admits.

We'll see about that. "What would my duties be as queen?"

"You will live here and, Ulf willing, you will bear my heirs. The grounds will be yours to explore. But not beyond that. It is not safe for Omegas."

"You have not made it safe for Omegas," I correct him.

Bestian looks thoughtful. "This is true. I have long suspected that there might be Omegas in my kingdom but if there are, they are hiding."

Like Ma, I realize.

"Tell me what you want, Rose."

Here we go. It's bargaining time. I had hoped it would come to this. "I will accept my role as your queen in exchange for one thing." I take a deep breath. "You will give Ma immunity for anything that she has ever done—or will do. You will never punish her. She will be pardoned officially, if necessary."

"Done." Bestian leans forward and props his elbows on the table. "In exchange, you will remain at my side. You will be my queen." He shifts, letting his gaze trail down my body as his voice deepens. "And you will bear my heirs."

There's a rush of liquid heat between my legs. Good grief, am I this affected by him just looking at me? I swallow. What have I gotten myself into?

"Tell me what you're thinking," Bestian demands.

"I'm processing. It's true, we are compatible—at least physically." I clear my throat. "But I barely know you."

"That is easily dealt with. Ask me anything, and I'll answer."

I steel myself. "What happened to your face? Why do you wear the mask?"

"I wear it so you can look on me without disgust, my little moonflower."

I'd never do that, I want to say. But I hold my tongue.

"While my parents ruled, the kingdom was prosperous and untouched by the Red Death. I was a young prince with everything to live for. Then the curse hit. A mysterious and terrible illness swept across Medela, leaving loss and destruction in its wake. Few were spared."

I wait, silently, for him to continue.

"We all worked together to find a cure, reaching out across all of Ulfaria for help. Many of the kings and their representatives sent potential remedies. The Demon King sent us a bottle of tablets. The advisors of our neighboring kingdom Arboron found an ancient scroll listing cures for various ailments and had it delivered to me." He pauses and takes a breath. "The Stone King also sent a potion. My father warned me of his treachery, said not to trust him, but I was a fool. I had so much pride. I was on a quest to cure the curse, and nothing would stop me. I wanted to be an ulfdamn hero."

My fingers are clenched around the stem of the goblet. I

force my hand to relax. "What happened next?" I say gently, when Bestian seems unwilling to continue.

He lets out a sigh. "I unsealed the Stone King's potion without protective measures. It released a poison gas which turned to acid, seeping into my pores. This was the result." He indicates the mask hiding most of his face. If I look closely at his uncovered skin, I can pick out a few scars where the acid bit into him.

"Why would the Stone King do that?" I ask. "Just sheer malice?"

"He was desperate for an Omega of his own, and happened to covet my mother, in particular." Bestian's voice is thick with rage. "He wanted to kill my father so he could take my mother as his—but he also wanted my father to suffer. He messed up, however. For one, I opened the bottle, not my father. And for another, the poison gas was slow-acting. Instead of killing me immediately, it gradually ate at my skin and spread through my body. Movement got increasingly difficult as I slowly turned into a living statue. The pain was indescribable. There was no doubt I was dying. Soon, the poison would reach my heart and make it stop."

My eyes have filled with tears but I blink them back. I want him to keep talking.

"The *whisps* saved me. I was alone in my lab, but they surrounded me, dosed me with a tincture, and put me into a coma."

Bestian's voice trails off. He stares into the distance, lost in memory.

"But you survived," I say, my voice breaking with emotion. "You're still here."

"I didn't know what had happened until my father woke me. He had especially waited a few days until I was more stable but when I opened my eyes, and saw him... I was in so much pain, so furious with myself for being so foolish, I took my anger out on him. I raged at him—I roared in his face, telling him to leave. I did not act like a prince. I was a beast." There's so much shame in his voice. He stops and takes a ragged breath. "Only later did I learn why he'd woken me. He'd come to say goodbye."

"He was sick too?" My heart aches for the tortured king sitting opposite me.

Bestian gives a single nod. He's still staring into the distance, his eyes glazed.

"You didn't know," I remind him.

"But I should have. The Red Death was spreading, killing all in its wake. It didn't discriminate between Alpha or Beta, rich or poor. I managed to survive but I'd failed to save my parents. To find a cure. I'd failed everyone."

"I thought you found the cure? What was the potion you sent to Ma and all the others?"

Bestian heaves a sigh. "It's an effective medicine, one of the treatments listed on the scroll Arboron sent us. It's what ultimately stopped the poison from reaching my heart. But it's not a cure. There is no cure, only a counter spell. Which is what my father used to stop the Red Death."

"I don't understand."

"As I mentioned to you before, there is magic in our blood. A symbiosis between an Alpha King and the land. A bond, if you will. My father worked out how to use it to reverse the curse." Bestian pauses and it's so quiet, I can hear the ocean waves crashing in the distance. "Even though I was no longer in acute danger, I was in so much pain, I begged the *whisps* to put me under once more. The next time I came to, my father was dead... and so was my mother. So many in our kingdom. But the curse was broken."

The wind wafts around me. It's not until Bestian rises

and comes to my side to offer a handkerchief that I realize there are tears sliding down my cheeks.

"Don't be sad, beautiful Rose." He kneels so we're at eye level, and dabs my face with the cloth.

I take it and finish the job. "What happened to the Stone King?" I manage a tiny smile. "Tell me he got his comeuppance, like in the movies."

"He's dead," Bestian admits. "Albeit not by my hand."

"I'm so sorry you were hurt. And that you lost your family."

"All things die."

"Don't say that. You don't have to pretend you have a stone heart. Not with me."

"My heart died with my parents. Only when you broke the spell around my castle and woke me from my slumber did it begin to beat again. You are my heart, Rose. That is why I need you by my side."

Please don't leave me. I hear it clearly, even if he doesn't say it aloud. My head is spinning.

I gaze into his eyes. They're more black than green.

"Come," he says, rising and offering his arm. I take it and he ushers me to the edge of the balcony. Instead of leading me to the stairs, he stands with me at the rail, looking down over the garden.

"Where are we going?"

"Do you trust me?"

I blow out a breath. "Yes," I say, because I do. I trust him more than I've ever trusted a man. Even if he is a growly, overbearing Alpha-hole most of the time.

He faces me and takes my hand. I let his huge one swallow mine. There's a twinkle in his eyes.

It takes me a second to realize that we're no longer standing on the balcony but on an invisible platform, rising above the garden.

"I wanted tonight to be perfect. I wanted to show you something beautiful, but there is nothing more beautiful than you. Your skin is like the midnight sky, your eyes are like stars," he tells me.

He waves a hand and the air in front of us ripples, turning opaque and reflecting back the image of a giant Alpha with a slender Somali-American woman beside him. She's wearing a crown.

"This is who you are," Bestian continues. "This is who you were born to be. The universe brought you to me. You were the only one who could break through my barriers and bring me to life. "

He brings my hand to his mouth and kisses my knuckles. The part of his jaw covered by the mask is cool to the touch but his lips are warm, and heat surges in my belly.

"Dance with me," he whispers.

I blink because we're hovering over the garden. The clusters of moonflowers are glowing in various shades of pink, red, and black.

A gust of wind flurries around my skirts, lifting the train. I step close to Bestian and he pulls me against him. We're eye to eye—but how? My feet should have left the ground. I look down to realize I'm standing on invisible cushions of wind. I'm face-to-face with the king, like his equal, with the wind supporting me.

I slide my arms around his shoulders.

I have been fighting so hard not to fall for Bestian, convincing myself it was all biological. That my feelings weren't real. Worrying that it wasn't safe to open up to him completely—to let him in.

But for the moment, I will allow myself to melt. I will allow myself to believe in magic. Because it's all around me, and ignoring it won't make it go away.

I'm floating high above a magical castle and dancing

with an alien king under five moons with an invisible wind supporting me. None of this is possible—and yet it's really happening.

So I close my eyes and rest my cheek on Bestian's shoulder. I let him swing me across a magical dancefloor suspended over a field of glowing moonflowers.

I surrender to it all. To him.

EIGHTEEN

THIS EVENING IS EVERYTHING I EVER WANTED—AND more. Rose floats in my arms, her face blissful and relaxed. The crown sparkles in her curls. She came to me, the Omega I had been dreaming of. She fought her way to my castle and broke the spell. And now she looks every inch a queen.

My queen.

I guide her in big sweeping steps across the invisible platform I've conjured for us. She snuggles against my chest and I realize I've started purring, a steady, soothing rumble.

"Rose," I murmur. She blinks up at me, her eyes cloudy with need.

"Bestian," she moans, and clamps her arms around my neck, pressing against me. She nuzzles my jaw. I avert my head before she tries to rub against my mask.

I order the wind to take us to her nesting room immediately. Rose doesn't seem to be aware of her surroundings anymore. Her estrus is consuming her, despite my attempt to soothe her with my purr.

By the time we reach the bed, she's arching against me and grinding her hips. The sweet musk of her slick rises to fill my senses. I groan, my cock throbbing.

She's fumbling with her gown, tugging the voluminous skirts up around her waist. She's not wearing any underwear and I reach for the hot, wet core of her, squeezing hard. Her clit is like a rigid jewel against my palm.

"Bestian!" Hot slick spurts rhythmically into my hand. She's coming already.

And she's calling my name.

Her head is tossed back, her eyes closed. Lost in the throes of pleasure. Her bare neck is mere inches away. So smooth. So tempting.

My canines lengthen, my mouth floods with saliva. It would be so easy to sink my throbbing teeth into her soft flesh. To make her mine. To claim her completely.

My purr grows into a growl. Rose shudders and gushes some more. "Please," she whimpers. "I need it. I need—" She reaches for me and I grasp her wrists, forcing her to turn face down on the bed, pushing her skirts higher up her waist.

"Naughty girl." I spank her, hard. She moans and raises her ass higher, for more. "Trying to command your king." After a couple more slaps, I delve my fingers between her slippery folds, making her shudder. "Is this what you want?" I find the spot that makes her writhe and stroke circles over her swollen, slick flesh.

"I want you. Please, Bestian..."

Her name on my lips is like a drug.

She slides her knees wider apart, pressing her shoulders into the bed to offer her cunt up to me. In the soft light of the bedroom, the crown gleams in her curls. Tugging off my clothes, I order a *whisp* to remove it so it doesn't bounce off and hurt her while I rut her. Once the ornament is safely on the bedside table, I grip my queen's thighs and spread them further, impossibly wide. My cock breaches her folds, driving into her slowly. The bedclothes muffle her moans.

Ulf, she feels so good around me. My canines are throbbing.

I thought this position would make it easier for me to resist giving her the claiming bite. But as soon as I'm knot-deep inside her, she arches up, pushing into my thrusts. Her head tips back. It would be so easy to thread my hand through her curls, tug her back, and sink my teeth into the tender junction between her shoulder and neck.

I grit my teeth and focus on the way her cunt is stretched around me. Rose tips her head to the side, offering a beautiful, bare expanse of skin. The urge to bite her is overwhelming, yet something holds me back. My body and my mind are at war.

With a roar of frustrated anger, I push her back down and cover her body with mine. My knot expands fully and Rose cries out, her tight heat rippling around my cock. Her climax triggers my own. As I shudder and throb, filling her with endless ropes of my cum, I angle my face away from the scented temptation of her flesh, and sink my aching teeth into a pillow instead.

***

The Queen's crown gleams in the darkness beside our bed. Rose slumbers beside me, her face tucked into my chest. I crane my head to scan the quiet corners of our bedroom. The *whisps* have removed the ruined pillow I bit into.

My shoulders ache with tension so I roll onto my back. Rose's pretty bow lips turn downwards in a pout. She reaches for me, her forehead wrinkling in sleep. Only when I draw her back into my arms does she settle with a sigh.

I hold her, admiring her in the gentle glow of the approaching dawn. My heir could be taking root in her belly even now. Khan's queen had a perfect baby girl, so we know that Ulfarri/human pairings can be successful. I never dreamed I might procreate before Rose appeared on my doorstep, and the idea now fills my heart with joy.

Last night, she came to me wearing the crown of a queen. She has agreed to assume her place beside me. She still cares for her Ma, but she is willing to leave her Ulfarri home behind, and stay here, with me.

The urge to give her the claiming bite—just a faint desire on our first night together—has become a raging, desperate need. But every time I'm just about to give in and actually do it, bind her to me completely, something stops me.

Rose is my queen. My mate. I could claim her at any time—but especially while we're

rutting—and she couldn't do a thing to stop me. So why haven't I marked her yet? Why didn't I claim her last night?

I shift my gaze again to look at her, drinking in her beauty, my thoughts whirling. How can someone so beautiful love a beast? Is it pity?

Is it not enough that I refused to let her leave and persuaded her to be my queen, chaining her to someone as monstrous as me? Must I also claim her with the bite, binding her body and soul to me, forever? The bond is so strong, she could never leave me. A blessing, but also a curse. After all, my parents' soul-bond was the reason my mother died...

I push those dark thoughts away to focus on Rose's face. I cannot let that happen to her. It would break me. But my basest instincts to claim my Omega will only grow stronger until I do it. Will I always be able to resist?

Rose jerks in my arms. Her sudden, sharp wail makes me jump. "No! Don't leave me!" she cries, and starts thrashing about as if running somewhere.

She's having another nightmare. In a flash, I've pulled her tighter against me. I stroke her damp forehead, my purr reverberating through us both. "Hush, my little moonflower, it's all right. You're safe. You're with me."

Usually, when I speak to comfort her in these situations, she stays asleep but her face relaxes and she settles down. This time, it's different. I almost jump out of my skin when her eyes fly open and she stares at me with a look of sheer agony that makes the hair on the back of my neck stand on end.

"Rose?" I whisper.

"He... he... left me," she manages, still looking at but somehow not really seeing me.

Then, burying her face in my chest, she bursts into tears.

Rose

Abandoned at the altar. Jilted bride. Runaway groom. Phrases straight out of descriptions for chick flicks, historical dramas, romance novels—and, apparently, my life.

It happened to me.

Bestian is purring but I'm so distraught that not even his usually reassuring rumble is doing much to soothe me right now.

I went through every agonizing second of that day in my dream in vivid, horrifying technicolor—waking up full of excitement and nerves, getting ready, the photographer, giggling with my smiling maid of honor—a friend from modeling. My estranged family wasn't invited so when I got to the church, my proud agent was the one who walked me down the long aisle towards the groom.

My fiancé.

Russell stood there in his suit, looking almost too handsome. Too shiny. Too perfect. But when I got close enough to really see his eyes, they were... blank. Devoid of the pride and love I had hoped to see. Chalking that up to nerves, I took my place beside him, in front of all our gathered friends and acquaintances, my bouquet trembling as I handed it to my maid of honor.

The officiant had barely begun to speak before Russell blurted out, "This is a mistake. I have to go. I can't marry you, Rose." While my world tilted on its axis and my heart shattered into a million pieces, he turned, strode briskly down the aisle, and was gone.

I rub my forehead. Did that really happen? To me? If so, how could I possibly have forgotten about it? Now, in the cold light of dawn, with Bestian clutching me tight, the humiliation is rolling over me in waves, hot and shameful. For Russell to wait until I was actually standing in the church with him, to reject me in front of pretty much everybody I knew—somehow, that betrayal was even worse than the loss of his love.

"Talk to me," Bestian says, his fingertips catching a tear as it spills over. "A bad dream?"

"Yes. But I don't think it was just a dream. I think it was a real memory."

"What happened?"

Part of me wants to confide in him. Then again, talking about it means reliving it. Again. And I want to forget it again as soon as possible. Not to mention, judging by the way he sometimes reacts whenever I so much as refer to having known a guy before him, Bestian might seethe with jealousy and I'll have to talk him down. I don't have the emotional capacity for that right now. I just want to stuff the whole thing back down into my subconscious.

"Rose?"

He sounds so concerned, I feel guilty for shutting him out. But the alternative is worse.

"Please," I whisper, "I don't want to talk about it."

"You said you trusted me." I can tell he's trying to stay calm but he sounds hurt.

"I know. And I do. It's just... too painful right now. You can understand that, right?"

"Who left you?"

His words make me jerk in his arms. "What?"

"You were crying out. You said that he left you. Who left you, Rose?"

Fuck. I must have been talking in my sleep. "That must have been a different dream or something," I lie. "I don't remember anyone leaving me." Bestian is so possessive, the thought of me pining for any other guy—even if those feelings are long gone—would drive him nuts.

There's a pause. I hold my breath, praying he won't question me any further. Then, "If you say so."

He's clearly not convinced but to my utter relief, he drops the topic—for now, at least.

"Thank you," I say aloud, snuggling closer to him. "For looking after me. For purring. It's very sweet."

"You were in distress," he says simply. "As I said before, I can't tolerate your pain."

"Pain is a part of life," I mutter but as I say that, it occurs to me that I've been spouting

these lines for god knows how long—trite, short, simple

phrases that fill self-help books and motivation materials—but I've never really thought about them.

"Yes, my little moonflower, but so is happiness. And I want to see you have so much more happiness than pain."

"I feel the same way about you. That's why I keep nagging you, you know. Telling you to step up and start ruling your kingdom the way you were meant to." The words are bubbling out of me, a welcome distraction from the nightmare. "I don't say it to make you feel guilty or ashamed."

"I know," he tells me. "My happiness has increased a thousandfold since you entered this castle. And I want to spend every moment with you. I'd have so much less time if I were an active ruler."

"Maybe, but you'd have a lot more confidence and belief in yourself. And I'm sure you could manage. The other kings with mates make it work somehow, right?"

"I assume so." Rolling onto his back, he pulls me with him until my head is resting right on his huge, bare chest. His fingers toy with my hair and he yawns. "Will you stay calm if I stop purring? I'm suddenly so very, very tired."

"Sure," I say. "If you want to go back to sleep, you don't need my permission."

"No, little one, but I want to make sure you're not still in distress. I could stay awake for you. I would stay awake for you."

"I don't doubt it. But honestly, I'm fine. You get some more sleep. I'll be right here—might doze off again myself."

His only reply is a soft half-snore. I force myself to relax against him and close my eyes but on the inside, I'm wide awake.

So, I got jilted at the altar. The man I loved enough to want to marry and spend the rest of my life with decided he'd be better off without me. I wonder what his reasons were.

Whether there even was a reason. Another woman? Secretly gay? Or did he just decide that he wasn't ready? If he ever told me, I can't remember.

God, the look on my agent's face. The worst part was, most of my so-called friends were actually Russell's. They chose him over me.

Why would my stupid, mean brain choose this memory to give me back—out of all the available options? All the happy moments, funny moments, touching moments I must have had over the years, things I would no doubt be delighted to relive—and yet this is the one that surges to the top of the list. It's so fucking unfair.

When I was younger, I adored tales of love, romance, and happily-ever-afters. I just assumed that I got more practical as I grew up, as many people do.

It turns out, that's not true. My constant inner resistance is due to fear, not cynicism. And really, is it any wonder, after what Russell did?

On a vague level, I already knew that guys had hurt me before. Dating is a tough game, and you can't always be a winner. But being rejected at the altar is a whole new level of anguish. Enough to put anyone off the idea of falling in love and risking that again.

I glance up at Bestian's strong jaw and breathe in his scent. We can be so good together, yet I'm not the only one holding something back. My body's sore from the rut. Between the knot and my constant orgasms, I'm wrung out. But instead of satisfaction, I'm aching. There's a snarl of distress in my heart that has nothing to do with the nightmare I just had.

I rub my cheek against his chest, wishing I could climb

inside him. I don't know what I need, but I know it's something only he can give.

Just listen to yourself, my inner cynic whispers. *What could you possibly need that only he could give? What more could you even want? You've agreed to be his queen, he gives you the best sex of your life, and he's utterly devoted to you.*

All good points, I guess. I close my eyes, my thoughts a whirling jumble. Last night really was magical in so many ways. The night sky, the moonflowers, my dress, the look on Bestian's face when he greeted me at the steps. How could I not believe in fairytales?

I'm right in the freaking middle of one.

NINETEEN

Bestian

THE ORB BEFORE ME IS BLINKING BRIGHTLY, SIGNALING an incoming communication. I ignore it for as long as I can, then finally wave a hand to allow the caller to speak to me.

It's Frex, one of my senior council members. I promoted him because although he's loquacious, he's more efficient than the rest of my father's council put together.

I still do not wish to talk to him.

"What?" I snarl.

"Your Majesty." Frex squints out of the orb at me, even though his orb should show nothing of my visage. I do not allow my councilors to see me. "I have news. King Aurus sends his congratulations on your new queen. Your new Omega queen."

I grunt.

"He sent a gift."

"Let me guess. It was big. And gold."

"And, for some reason, shaped like a *tyrlee*."

"What?"

"A *tyrlee* is a four-legged beast of burden. Often used to

ride upon, especially in the Forest Kingdom, where Alphas ride them to hunt. The *tyrlee's* milk is also a good source of—"

"I know what a *tyrlee* is," I snap. Ulf give me patience. "Why did Aurus send me a golden statue of one?"

"We have not been able to decipher the reason. The note attached by King Aurus mentioned it was his queen's idea. We do know that it is hollow."

Damn Aurus and his mind-games.

The councilor continues, "The Golden Queen also sent along her own gift—a glow orb in a peculiar shape. Her note said it was a *lava lamp*, and she hoped your queen would appreciate the gift. I presume the giving of *lava lamps* is an important human custom. Both gifts should arrive at your residence tomorrow."

"Very well." Rose will be pleased to have something from her people. Which reminds me, I must set up a meeting between her and the other human Omegas. Maybe this gift exchange will be a good introduction.

Frex clears his throat. "When do you wish to announce the coronation?"

"Never. There won't be one. There is no need."

"But the queen—"

"I never had a coronation. And I am still king, correct?"

"Yes, Your Majesty. But the people are curious. It would be—"

"My mind is made up," I interrupt him. "Now, is there anything else?"

"Surely you plan to at least come to Medea City. So when can we expect to see you here?"

"Never." None of my subjects will see my face again. They knew me as a prince. As a king, I have always ruled from afar, and I will continue to do so. The sooner they understand this, the better.

"Very well." Frex sounds sorrowful. "There is one final matter."

"What is it?" I snap.

"The Red Death. Many have recovered, but we're getting reports that some are relapsing. We fear the curse might be spreading again."

No. This is my worst nightmare come true. "Quadruple the number of magicians researching it. There has to be a cure. We will find it."

"At once, Your Majesty."

I end the communication, my head spinning. The Red Death has returned. And if people are relapsing, there's a chance my medicine will no longer help them. Damn the Stone King and his evil magic... tormenting us even after his death.

A small orb displays a copy of my parents' portrait on my desk. Even here, my father's eyes are on me, reminding me of his last words to me.

When I am gone, you must take my place as king. Work every day to prove yourself worthy. Rule well, my son.

I wonder what he would do if he'd known the Red Death would come again? Would he have made the same choices, knowing his sacrifice would be in vain?

I flick my fingers and the orb goes dark. My parents' image disappears.

I long to see Rose but I have work to do. I tried to cure the curse, so far I have failed. But I cannot stop trying. The fate of the kingdom rests in my hands, even if I am unworthy to rule them.

I'm in my study, which is now my favorite place in the palace. It helps that everything here is a little closer to my size. I feel less like Goldilocks.

Bestian has been incredibly busy lately, too busy to spend time with me. At first, I thought he was giving me a chance to recover from my last, draining cycle of estrus, but now it's been days since we spent any quality time together. At night, I go to sleep alone, in the morning, I wake up with a still-warm, Bestian sized-dent in the bed beside me. I know he holds me while I sleep, which soothes me somewhat. He hasn't completely abandoned me. I should be grateful for the reprieve, but it's left me wanting. I never thought I'd miss his overbearing presence, but I do. When I encouraged him to be more of a king, I didn't expect him to go from one extreme to the other.

Be careful what you wish for, as they say.

In the meantime, I've been settling in. Learning the castle, making the study my own. The *whisps* helped me change out some of the decor. The lava lamp one of the human Omega queens sent me sits in a corner.

What a weird, random-ass gift. Bestian seemed to think the lava lamp was a symbolic gesture. He acted like I'd know what human custom Kim was following. The only thing I can come up with is that this Kim lady wants to get high with me and listen to the Dark Side of the Moon album backwards.

Which is fair. I don't miss a ton about Earth, but I'm still keen to hang with another human. So far, Bestian's been too busy to arrange it.

There's a rush and a *whisp* deposits a fresh stand of sweet cakes beside me. The *whisps* have taken delight in making the dessert in all sorts of different flavors, to see what I like best. The three plates hold cakes in bright pink, velvety black, and acid green. I'm not sure what the hell sort of fruits or berries or nuts create those colors, but the hot pink one is very good.

I've been reading the history of Omegas, and it's fascinating. My favorite treatise is the one written by an Omega healer who worked in one of the convents. When Omega birth rates plunged, the Kings' Council decided to sequester Omegas in hidden, hard-to-reach fortresses, and instituted a lottery. The Omegas were hurried away to the fortresses as soon as they reached sexual maturity, and were kept there until they were assigned a mate—usually a high-ranking Alpha, a king, or a head warrior who could breed more sons.

Bestian told me the convents were real. At one point during his father's reign, Alpha warriors stormed them in defiance of the lottery. But they found them empty. The Omegas and their Beta guards had all disappeared.

It's fascinating history, and it's also giving me a knowledge of herbal lore. There are whole chapters on what herbs and nutrients are best for Omegas, to support their estrus cycles, increase fertility, ease pregnancy ailments, and so on. Ma would love it. I haven't yet asked to talk to her again, but I will soon.

"Hello?" An unseen voice makes me jump. Someone is speaking in the corner of this room. It continues in a nasal American accent, "Can you hear me now?"

I leap to my feet. The *whisps* whip around me. "What is that? Where is it coming from?"

There's a squawk like from a radio, and the voice says, "Emma? Emma! You're on mute."

"I'm not," another voice answers. This one has a softer, more distinguished tone. Sounds British. God, it's so good to hear my native language being spoken again without that stupid translator chip dubbing everything. I bite my lip.

"Your picture's off," the American replies. It's a small, tinny sound, and the speaker sounds female. "Can you hear me? You're on mute again."

The voices are coming from the lava lamp. I approach it.

"Hello?" I call. "Is someone there?"

"Kim, are you sure this is going to work?" Miss British accent—Emma—inquires.

I tip my head towards the lamp. "Hello? Can you hear me?"

"Shhh," Kim says. "I think I can hear her. Hello? Human?"

"I'm here," I say. "How are you doing this?"

"I hacked a communication orb. I'm Kim," the American says brusquely. "Good to meet you."

"I'm Emma," the British woman adds. "Good to meet you."

There's a pause. They're waiting for me to answer. "Um, thanks. I'm Rose," I speak into the lava lamp, feeling ridiculous. "You guys are the other humans?"

"Guilty," Kim says. "We're two of the humans brought here and given the special serum to turn us into Omegas. You know about that?"

"Yes."

"Awesomesauce. I'm mated to the Golden King, and Emma's with the Wanderer King."

"His name is Khan," Emma puts in.

"And there's one other human we know of, named Haley. She's mostly offline. She and the Hunter King like to go off and commune with the wilderness or something. Look, I can't talk long. But Emma and I wanted to make contact and make sure you're okay."

"Um, thank you. I'm good," I say. "I was hoping I'd get to speak to you."

"You're mated to the Beast King?" Emma asks.

"I don't know about *mated*," I say. This is the weirdest girls' chat I've ever had. "We're living together."

"That's how it starts," Kim says. "One day, you're living in the harem with the concubines, teaching them about orgasms, and the next, you're claimed by a giant Alpha. Emma's got a purple one. I've got a shiny gold one—like a life-sized Emmy statue but, you know, with an actual dick."

"Kim, please," Emma says, sounding prim. "TMI."

"Who else can I talk to about this stuff? You're my only friends. My only *human* friends. I hang out with a bunch of Beta nerds, but you guys can actually get my Earth jokes."

"Wait," I say. "Do you know how we got here?"

"Not really." Kim doesn't sound too fussed. "They refer to their scientists and engineers as magicians. In any case, they worked out it was something to do with portals and wormholes or something. There are at least four of us here— you, me, Emma, and Haley."

"There might be more," Emma puts in. "The kings are searching for them."

"Right. We don't know if more of us were brought over. It's all way too complicated to get into right now, but it boils down to a space experiment program gone wrong."

"Okay," I say. "Sounds like something out of Mystery Science Theater."

"See?" Kim crows. "I love hearing modern Earth references. In any case, we're all from the same time, and roughly the same area. I don't really remember my life before but Emma has a theory that she came through a portal that opened up in Richmond, Virginia."

"Richmond, Virginia... that sounds vaguely familiar," I say. I did travel a lot for my job.

"Do you remember much of your old life, Rose?" Emma asks.

"Just vague bits and pieces. I worked a lot when I wasn't studying. Didn't have much of a life. I had a lot of house plants."

"Fair enough," Kim says. "I think I just played video games all the time."

"Do you like the Beast King?" Emma asks. "Is he treating you well?"

"Yes," I answer. "He can be an overbearing asshole, but he's trying."

"That's good," Emma says.

"All Alphas are overbearing assholes. It's part of their DNA. Unfortunately, our Omega sides seem to find it hot." Kim sighs. "I practically begged Aurus to claim me."

"I did beg Khan," Emma mutters.

"Claim you?" I ask, feeling hesitant. "That's part of the... bond thing, right?"

"In a way. The bond is brought on by the claiming bite. Your Alpha literally bites you, making you his forever. It's like their version of marriage—only there's no divorce. As scary as it sounds, it feels amazing," Kim says.

"Has your king claimed you yet?" Emma asks.

I take a deep breath. There's a sad, gnawing feeling in my chest. "No. Not yet."

"I'm sure he will soon," Emma says.

"Yeah, I'm sure he's just making sure you want it," Kim adds.

Is he? I do—I think. All those times I tipped my head to the side, baring my neck to him, my Omega side was begging for the claiming bite. I just didn't know what I was asking for.

But Bestian knew. He had to have known. He's a nerd about this stuff, he can't be as clueless as I am. Does this mean he doesn't want to claim me? Maybe he doesn't feel what I feel.

A cold wind passes through my heart. If Bestian doesn't want to claim me... it doesn't bear thinking about. His rejection would be even worse than Russell leaving me at the altar.

"Besides," Kim is saying. "You guys just met, and you've been through a lot—"

"Khan and I had just met," Emma says. "It's an instinct thing—"

"Yeah, but that's Khan. Rose's guy is different. They're all different, in their ways. It took a while to get Aurus's head on straight, he kept sticking me in with the other concubines—"

"His what?" I ask, not sure I heard correctly.

"He had a whole bunch of concubines. A harem of them. I think he liked to pretend they were Omegas. He kept claiming I was one of them. I nixed that idea pretty quickly, but it still took a while before he officially claimed me, marking me as his queen."

"Your king doesn't have any concubines, does he?" Emma asks.

"Oh hell, no." But that could change. There were plenty of Ulfarri females eager to meet him at the Queen Covenant.

"I wouldn't worry about it too much, Rose," Kim says. "Maybe, if you want to, you could claim him. Give him a big old bite on the shoulder. Show him he belongs to you."

"I guess," I mutter. She makes it sound so easy.

"I'm sure he's just busy," Emma soothes. "I've heard your kingdom is struggling right now with the spread of a plague of some sort? A curse?"

My stomach drops down to my toes. "The Red Death? But... I thought that was cured."

"Khan told me the neighboring kingdoms to Medela have stopped all trade at the border, just to keep it from spreading. But maybe I'm mistaken?"

There's a roaring in my ears. Could it really be true? Could the Red Death be back? Again? I shiver. "I have to go."

"Of course," Emma says. "It was good to meet you, Rose."

"And now we have a way to check in with each other," Kim adds.

"Yes, thank you, lovely to meet you too," I say, rubbing my arms. Rogue brings me a cloak and I wrap it around myself gratefully. The chill has spread through me. My fingers and toes are freezing.

"Till next time!" Kim calls. "End communication." The lava lamp goes dark.

I pull the cloak tighter around my shoulders and hurry out of my study and through the Queen's lush gardens. The waterfall crashes in the distance as I exit the gallery and march down the corridor, my cloak streaming out behind me. Orbs light up as I pass.

The door to Bestian's study is closed. I've tried not to disturb him, even though he's obviously avoiding me, but right now, I don't give a fuck if I'm intruding.

"Open," I bark, and the door glides open like I've said the magic words.

Bestian is standing bent over his table, studying something, his back to me. Need rushes through me at the sight of him. I suck in deep gulps of his scent, but reach for my rage.

"Just when exactly were you going to tell me the Red Death is spreading again?"

Bestian straightens, but keeps his back to me. Tension radiates from the lines of his body. "Rose," he snarls.

"Yep. I'm surprised you remember me." I cross my arms over my chest. "It's been so long since you've seen me."

"I am busy. I do not wish to be disturbed."

"Too damn bad. Look, I'm not so fussed that you've retreated from me. After all, that's what you do, isn't it? Hide away? But I don't have time for your cowardice."

"Cowardice?" he whispers, his voice vibrating with menace.

"You heard me. A little wind just told me the Red Death is spreading again. If that's true, why haven't I been informed?"

"It is none of your concern!"

"Not my concern?" A pang of guilt hits me, mingling sickeningly with my outrage. Ma. I should have been paying more attention, been more diligent about making sure she was okay. This is what happens when you get swept up in some stupid fairytale romance. "Maybe you want to hide up here and pretend everything's great, but some of us don't spend our entire lives running from our responsibilities."

His head turns slightly, but he still doesn't look at me. "You think I'm *running*?"

"Yes." I cross the room to him and speak directly to his broad, rigid back. "Running and hiding like you always do."

"Get out." His voice is low. Dangerous.

"I'm not going anywhere."

He stiffens and for a moment I think he's going to roar, to rock the room with his unearthly, spell-ridden command. But instead he slowly and deliberately swivels to face me, revealing his ruined features in all their naked glory. The left side of his jaw and part of his cheek are smooth, showing a princely mien. The rest is ravaged, the skin pitted and melted like it was held over flames.

"Is this what you wanted to see?" he snarls, his emerald eyes blazing in his monstrous face. "Are you happy?"

I want to speak but my voice has deserted me. I lick my lips. There's such rage in his twisted expression. Rage, and pain.

"Is this what you wanted to prove?" He prowls towards me and seizes my upper arms. "How revolting I am? How unworthy I am of your love? Is this what you want me to admit?" He releases me to gesture to his face. "It is cowardice to keep this from you? To hide the fact that you have committed yourself to a beast?"

"Bestian," I croak. My hand hovers in the space between us; inches from the acid-ravaged skin.

He turns away. "Go. Just go. Leave me."

Finally, I find my voice. "Is that what you want?"

"It is what you prefer. I see it in your face."

The door behind me creaks. Rogue is there, waiting, holding its breath.

"You don't know me, Bestian. And it's obvious you don't know yourself. Maybe one day, you will see yourself as I see you. I can only hope so." Without giving him a chance to respond, I whirl and stalk out through the open door.

I leave the beast in his lair.

TWENTY

Rose

I STRIDE THROUGH THE PALACE, THE BREEZE WHIPPING the cloak around my heels. "He wants me to go?" I mutter to myself. "Fine. I'll go. But I won't abandon him."

I pause in the gallery, under Bestian's parents' portrait. "Your son is an idiot," I tell them. "But it's okay. I know just the thing to snap him out of this. I'll go check on Ma, and give him some space to get over his..." I wave a hand, "whatever *that* was."

An orb floats over to me from the alcove. Its surface reflects a view of Ma's cottage.

"No." I wave a hand and it halts. "I'm going to go see her myself. In person. I'll need a satchel or something. A waterskin, and some food—something hearty for the hike down. Sweet cakes." I stop to chew my lip. "I guess you can help me get whatever else Ma needs, right?"

Rogue flurries around my hair, reworking my elaborate, bejeweled hairdo into sensible braids. It replaces the crown but I pull it off and hold it out. "Take this. Keep it somewhere safe. I'll be back."

Outside, the day is cool. I pull my cloak around my shoulders. These past few days, the heat has lessened. The moonflowers are fading.

Rogue catches up, dropping a heavy satchel onto my shoulder.

"Thanks. You're coming, right?"

The *whisp* plays with the ends of my braids.

"Good. I'll need your help breaking the magic boundary so I can get out of here."

I've almost made it to the wall when a roar shakes the palace behind me.

Perfect timing.

I lengthen my strides. "Faster," I whisper to the *whisp*. "Can you make me go faster?"

With my next step, my foot lands on an invisible platform. On instinct, I throw out my hands but I'm perfectly balanced—the wind is lifting me. Under my foot there's nothing but air.

I take a few more steps like I'm climbing invisible stairs, each stride amplified by the buoyant wind. The wall looms a few feet in front of me.

"Rose," Bestian bellows.

I bound forward and soar over the wall. There's a slight tingle—that must be the boundary spell—and I've cleared the top, gasping as electricity zings through me, dancing down the hillside, twenty feet in the air.

Holy shit. I can fly!

"Rose," Bestian roars again, his voice crackling with desperation.

I glance over my shoulder to see him soar over the wall after me, his own cloak streaming out behind him. His hood is up but his face is bare.

My heart pounding, I whirl in midair, and fly faster. Up ahead is the valley, with the village nestled in the hillside's shadow. I zigzag, changing course, and head for the sound of the waves. Beyond the castle's cliff is a frothy surf and a long blue-gray swath of sea.

There's a sandy strip between the jagged cliff-face and the water. I head for it, racing over the invisible, wind-made road.

Bestian's shouts are growing louder. He's gaining ground.

The king told me to run but then he chased me. Should I let him catch me?

A wave of his scent assails my senses, carried across by the breeze. My tummy twists in a now-familiar flip of longing. Even when I'm not in estrus, I want him.

I'm twenty feet from the sand when he cannonballs into me, surrounding me with his warm bulk. We tumble together, plowing into a bank of warm air. The wind beneath us is softer than any cushion.

Bestian tears at his cloak until it flies free and floats down to spread out on the dry sand. Slowly, the wind lowers us to the ground.

I wriggle until I'm face to face with him. He grabs my wrists and pins me on my back, covering me with his huge body. "Rose."

I'm breathless, my heart racing with excitement and desire. "Bestian."

"I'm so sorry I spoke to you that way," he says. "I'm a fool. A big, ugly fool."

"You're not ugly," I whisper. "That's what I was trying to tell you."

He heaves out a sigh. "Don't leave," he says. "Don't leave me."

"I'm not leaving, dumbass." I wrap my legs around him. "I'm here. I'm with you." I free a hand to palm his scarred cheek. "I'm here."

His mouth crashes down over mine, kissing me on and on until I'm breathless and the aching throb in my clit has become unbearable.

"Please," I whisper, "fuck me."

His answering growl makes me tingle all over. Passionate, breathless, we roll over on the sand, tugging at each other's clothes, baring ourselves just enough so he can get inside me. For a second I panic, worried I won't be able to take him if I'm not in estrus, but he goes slow. He turns me on so much, I'm more than wet enough, groaning with pleasure as he finally slides home. We make love without words, drinking each other in, and when we reach that dizzying pinnacle, we do it together.

Afterwards, we collapse on Bestian's cloak, panting. I'm snuggled against his chest. His heart is thumping beneath my cheek. My pussy is still fluttering with tiny aftershocks, but that niggling sense of dissatisfaction has returned. I decide to give it a voice.

"Why won't you claim me?" I murmur. I bared my neck to him again just now, and once again, he ignored it. The feeling of rejection is acute.

"I will never claim you," he says.

I stiffen and move to pull away but he catches my shoulder and tugs me back.

"Rose, no, you don't understand."

Hot tears sting my eyes. "If you think you're going to get a bunch of concubines while *I'm* your queen, you can—"

"Concubines? What? What are you talking about? I would never do that. I would never need to." He props himself up over me, settling a huge hand on my chest, over my collarbone. Its heavy warmth soothes me. "You are the only one for me."

"Then why not bind us both together forever? Doesn't

the bite mean I can never leave you? I would've thought you'd be all over that." I manage a tiny smile.

Bestian is silent but there's a world of hurt in his eyes.

I reach up and trace my fingers over the ridges of his scars. "Is it because of this? Because I don't care. I swear."

He huffs. "It's not that. It is not *only* that," he amends and rolls away, coming to a sitting position. "Rose, there's something you should know."

I rise too, and climb into his lap. His expression is distant and it makes me want to be close to him.

"There is great power in the bond between two souls," Bestian says, his eyes more gray than green, matching the endless ocean. "But with it comes danger." He lets out a ragged breath. "My reason for not claiming you fully... it has to do with my parents. How they died. How... I killed them."

Oh, Bestian. I steel my features and nod. "Tell me."

"The day we first heard of the Red Death, my father was adamant that we stop it. We were all scholars. We would search high and low for a cure. But my father knew that there was a way to stop it instantly. A failsafe."

Bestian reaches over and touches one of my braids. When Rogue did my hair, it took out the jewels, but it seems one got missed. Bestian plucks it out and turns it this way and that, making it wink red and black and purple in the fading light.

"I told you of the symbiosis between an Alpha King and the land. It is a power Alpha kings have, to bond with the land. We don't understand it, but my father studied it all his life, and he understood more than most. It is within the king's power to draw strength from the land. And, conversely, to draw out curses and heal the land by taking those onto himself. When the Red Death first started spreading, my father wanted to do that right away. But he didn't."

"Why not?"

"Because I stopped him. It was my stupid pride. I did not know if drawing the curse into himself would harm him. I argued with him. I said there was another way. I was so sure..."

Bestian trails off and stares out over the water. He looks so lost, I mold a palm to his face, to warm his skin. To bring him back to me.

"We threw ourselves into searching for a cure. Days and weeks passed, and things grew worse. People were dying. My own mother started showing symptoms. But I *knew* I could find the answer. I could fix it."

"Bestian," I murmur.

He blinks and says in a different voice, a more scholarly one, "I suspect now that the Stone King cast the curse. It caused him great harm—there is a rebound, a recoil to such curses—and I believe casting it weakened him and poisoned his land in return. But at the time, we did not know that. So when the Stone King sent a parcel, claiming it was a possible cure, I opened it just like I did the others." He grimaces. "If I were really wise, I would have listened to my father, who warned me countless times how evil the Stone King was. I would never have opened it. But I was working day and night, visiting my sick mother instead of sleeping, poring over ancient scrolls... I was desperate. And in the end, it was all for nothing. I destroyed my face and nearly died. And my parents paid the ultimate price."

I take a moment to absorb it all. To think. "You said you were responsible for their deaths," I say. "How could you be at fault, if you lay dying?"

"I let my hubris and my pride get the better of me. Don't you see? Because of me, because I was so sure I could find a better solution, my father waited to reverse the curse and take it into himself. By then, the afflicted numbered in the hundreds of thousands. The entire kingdom was suffering. My father pulled all that into himself, and it was too much. Too big. It killed him instantly—and, through him, my mother as well. They both died because of me."

My face must show that I don't understand because Bestian explains further, "My father claimed my mother the usual way. They were soul-bonded forever. When he cast the spell to break the curse, he took it into himself." His voice is barely a whisper now, ragged with grief. "He couldn't have known... but when he did that, my mother absorbed it too, through the soul-bond." He lowers his head, staring at the sand. "I killed them both."

"You didn't."

"I did. My father wanted to absorb the curse right in the beginning, when there were few more than a thousand cases. But I argued against it. I assured him I could find a cure. Find another way. If he hadn't waited... he and my mother would have lived. So many more would have lived!" His roar of anguish echoes off the cliff-face.

My heart aches for him. "You don't know that. You don't know it wouldn't have killed him anyway. And you said your mother was already sick. Dying." I take his head between my hands. "Bestian, listen. Your parents made their own decisions. They died for their kingdom. They died so that you and others might live. Your father did what he thought was best. And so did you."

He's silent for a long time, his face buried in his hands. When he looks up, his eyes are glistening. "Hopefully now you understand. That is why I will not claim you. It could be a death sentence." He grips my shoulders, his claws lightly pricking my skin. "I can't lose you, Rose. I won't. Ever."

"You won't. I'm here. I wasn't leaving for good. I only wanted to check on Ma. And… okay, a part of me wanted to run, so you would chase me. Which worked." I grin at him, but he's too serious to smile. I slide my fingers over his marred skin to trace his beautiful lips. "I do understand why you haven't claimed me. I only asked for it because a part of me needs it… wants it." I hold my breath for a moment and then ask, "Do you feel the same?"

His groan reverberates through us both. "Oh, my little moonflower. I cannot describe the depth of my desire to claim you properly. It is beyond words. I've come so close so many times. But I value your life above all else. Better to live as two souls in two bodies, than one soul and risk your death."

I stroke his thick, glossy hair. "You care for me."

"Yes." He sighs and lets his forehead fall against mine.

"This is the Bestian I know. You're a grumpy Alpha-hole, but deep down, you care."

"Thank you, Rose."

I pause. I need to ask the next question but I'm afraid of the answer. "With the curse starting to spread again now… will you be able to heal the land? As your father did?"

"I don't know. My father sacrificed himself for our kingdom. As I told you before, he woke me—when it was clear I would survive the acid attack. He stood beside my bed and told me he didn't blame me. I was out of my mind with pain, raving. He said he forgave me." Bestian takes a deep breath. "He told me I would one day be king, and there would come a time when I must prove I am worthy of ruling. And when that time came, he knew I would do the right thing."

"He was right," I whisper. "You will. You are the king."

I shiver in the sudden chill. Bestian frowns and scoots us both onto the sand so the wind can lift his cloak and drape it around me. "We should go before the tide comes in," he says.

"I want to see Ma."

Bestian hesitates. "Just after you left, I asked the *whisps* for a report. I'm sorry to tell you this... but Matron is ailing. Leelah is with her. She thought it was just exhaustion, but it is possible the curse is upon her again..."

Oh, no. Please, God... I bite my lip, fighting back a torrent of emotions—fear for Ma, sadness about the curse and all the devastation it has wrought, and anger at Bestian for waiting this long to tell me.

"I am so sorry, Rose," he says. His eyes are haunted, he looks wrung out.

"It's not your fault," I say. Yelling at him now won't fix anything. "But I must go to her—immediately."

"Of course." Bestian rises, lifting me with his usual ease, and setting me on my feet "You must."

Rogue whirls around me, wrapping me in new clothes: loose, soft pants and a tunic, sturdy enough for travel.

"The wind will take you straight to her cottage," Bestian says.

"Thank you." I hesitate. I would ask him to come with me but after everything he's just told me, would visiting Ma be like watching his parents die again?

I immediately shove that thought aside. I won't think of Ma dying. I can't.

"It'll be all right," I say briskly. "I'll visit her, and when she's better, I'll come back to you." The moment I finish my sentence, the wind lifts me up. I float up and away, leaving Bestian standing, his head bowed, barefoot on the beach.

"Go now, little one." His voice is weary. Strained. Broken. "Remember me when the moonflowers blossom and glow."

The wind carries me back to Ma's cottage, setting me

down just outside the gate. "Thank you," I whisper, because I was raised to be polite, even when I'm almost beside myself with worry.

Dusk has fallen. The vines retreat as I walk down the path. The glowing moonflowers light the way.

The cottage door creaks open at my touch, and the dense, familiar scent of herbs greets me. The fire in the downstairs hearth has burned down to a few glowing embers, and as I enter, Rogue rushes past me to stoke it. "Thank you," I tell it. More logs float into the grate, and the fire crackles happily.

"Ma?" I call softly, in case she's sleeping. "I'm here."

Footsteps sound upstairs and a shadowy shape appears on the top step. "Rose?" The voice is younger than Ma's. The fire flares up and in the fresh flood of light, I make out a familiar face.

"Leelah. Is everything all right? Is Ma—" I hold my breath, unable to say it. What if I'm too late?

"She's here." Leelah steps back as I come up the stairs. "She's... come see for yourself."

I squeeze her shoulder as I pass.

Ma's bedroom is dark but Rogue flows past me, lighting a few candles around the bed. The glow illuminates Ma's haggard face.

A spear of ice travels down my spine. "Ma?"

Her eyelids flutter but remain closed. I sit and take her hand—her skin is hot to the touch. Her lips are cracked. The scarlet rash has spread over her face, but a spot on her high cheekbone is turning ash gray.

A rustle just beyond the doorway tells me Leelah is hovering in the hall.

"What's happening to her?" I ask without taking my eyes off Ma. "What is this?"

"It's the curse," Leelah whispers. "She was doing so

much better, I thought she'd been cured—until earlier today. I was visiting, and she sounded tired. She said she might turn in early. When I came to check on her, she was burning up with fever. And then..." She comes to stand beside me. "See that, on her cheek? The skin turns hard. This happens in the final stages of the Red Death. The victims... turn to stone."

The dread is making me numb. "What about the medicine the king sent?"

"She's taken it all."

"I can get more—"

"Even if you could, she can't take any more," Leelah says softly. "She can't drink it. There's nothing we can do. She's beyond healing now, Rose." Her voice is thick with sorrow.

"No," I whisper. "No. Get me more medicine," I order Rogue. "Get me anything... anything in the king's possession that might help. We have to help her!"

My braids fly back as the *whisp* puffs past me. The window sails upward and the shutters clatter.

"It's okay," I tell Leelah, who's shrunk back in the corner, her hands clutched to her breast. "It's just Rogue. One of the king's magical servants." I turn back to Ma, settling onto a stool and taking her hand. "It's all right, Ma. You'll be okay. Help is on the way."

"Rose?" Leelah asks in a small voice.

"Yes?"

"Is it true? Are you the Omega chosen in the Queen Covenant? Did you meet the king?"

"Yes. But that's not important now. I'm here. I'm home. Everything will be all right."

I just wish I was as certain as I sound.

TWENTY-ONE

Bestian

Would I have done it all over again?

Yes.

In a heartbeat.

If I had known then what I know now, I like to think I would have behaved differently—but regret is easy when you're looking back.

Rose... my little moonflower... my perfect mate and my true love... she was in my life for such a brief, dazzling time, yet she changed everything.

When I stood on the beach watching her float away from me, I hoped and prayed that she would feel my love for her. I was too cowardly to say it aloud.

I stand in my study with my hands braced on my desk, my claws digging into the wood as I stare at the orb through a watery gaze. The anguish in my chest is so intense, I can't breathe.

She promised to return once she'd nursed the healer back to health, but we both know the truth. The Red Death is deadly. Some were saved when I sent the medicine, but the chance of her Ma recovering after a relapse... it's not worth calculating. Not worth dwelling on.

Would Rose ever return to me if I let her Ma die? Ever forgive me?

Questions I'll never know the answer to. It doesn't bear thinking about.

One way or another, that moment on the beach was a goodbye.

If you're the king, you should do something. Your people are dying... It's time to wake up and help them.

There's only one way to save my kingdom. My people. To make amends for all my wrongs.

There's a vase on my desk that holds a single, wilting moonflower. I touch a petal and it floats softly into my hand.

Will you heal the land? As your father did?

My parents' faces glow in the orb beside the vase. My father's eyes are intense, sorrowful.

The time will come when you must prove you are king, he told me long ago. I barely heard him through the haze of pain, but I can hear him now. *I know you, my son. You will do the right thing.*

"Soon," I tell him and my mother. *Soon, I will join you.*

I take a deep breath, and leave my study. Prowling through the castle, I give the *whisps* their final commands before releasing them into the world. In every room, the windows and doors swing open and as I pass by, the vines swarm in. It is time.

I come to a halt in the ballroom at the foot of the stairs, where Rose stood when she first breached my walls and entered my palace. This will be my final resting place. The vines will creep in and consume every last stone. One day, there will be nothing left but a wilderness.

I sink down onto the bottom step, allowing myself one last memory of Rose. The way she felt in my arms. Her intoxicating scent. Her smooth skin. The look in her beautiful eyes when she stood at the top of this very staircase and gazed down at me.

The pain is so sharp, so acute, that whatever happens next will be a blessed relief.

I take a deep breath and exhale it slowly. As I do so, I extend my magic—my power and birthright—out beyond the castle bounds. I release the boundary magic, the barrier between myself and the world, the spell I wove when I awoke alone in a castle haunted by my parents' ghosts.

My kingdom is hurting—I can feel it now. The ache intensifies in my body, sparks of fire in my fingertips swiftly spreading. My groan creaks out of me. The rash spreads swiftly, a scarlet tide crawling over my body. The curse burns like a thousand flames licking at my skin, and yet the pain is nothing compared to the agony in my heart.

I am dying as I have lived—all alone. It's better this way. At least Rose is gone, so she won't have to witness this, my final sacrifice. It is my hope that she will live a long, happy life with the healer, and remember me when the moonflowers blossom and glow.

Beneath the angry scarlet rash, my flesh crackles and turns ash gray. My fingers and toes harden first, my limbs follow suit. I can do nothing but sit here as my body turns into stone. The final stage of the Red Death. With excruciating slowness, the rot creeps towards my heart.

How long has it been since Rose left? An hour? A day? A week?

An eternity.

I send a silent plea to Ulf to hurry things up. To put me out of my misery. I don't know how much more of this I can stand, and yet I have no choice.

I am suffering the same fate my father did. It seems

fitting. I would smile at the irony but I can no longer move my face.

I can only hope my sacrifice isn't in vain.

The king can heal the land.

For too long, I neglected my responsibilities. My endless shame and grief kept me in the shadows, hiding from the people I was born to protect and lead. Now it's too late. I will never have the chance to rule over a happy kingdom as my father did, but for once in my life, in this very moment, I can be the king he wanted me to be. The king he believed I could be.

The king Rose believes I am.

Soon.

Rose

A breeze caresses my cheek, waking me. Rogue. I stayed up all night by Ma's bedside, bathing her fevered brow, willing the stone-gray scales to retreat from her skin. Leelah made endless cups of tea and mixed tinctures until she was swaying on her feet—I finally sent her home to sleep. Rogue and I took over. I hovered over Ma as the *whisp* fetched what it could to help me.

At some point, I must have passed out on my stool, my face smooshed against the bed.

I raise my head. The window is open and the vines have crept in. The moonflowers' glow is fading with the dawn. The dark blossoms' heads droop, their petals floating to the floor. They're withering before my eyes.

Something glitters in the candlelight—a flash of jewels gleaming amid the bedclothes an inch from my fingertips. I frown and am just reaching for it when Ma's hand settles over mine.

She turns her head and her lips part. "Rose?

"Ma?"

She squints at me. Her eyes are clear. "Is that you? I dreamed—"

"It's me," I manage, my throat tight. "I'm here." I squeeze her hand lightly. "How are you feeling?"

A smile touches her lips. "I'm better."

An earthenware cup of water floats past me and towards her. I help her take a sip. She drinks it all greedily, and reaches for the mug of steaming, sweet tea that Rogue brings next.

"Help me up," she says, her voice sounding stronger. I rush to prop pillows behind her. "Been in this bed too long," she mutters—and that's when I know she'll be okay.

Overwhelmed with exhaustion and relief, I burst into great, gulping sobs.

"Rose?" Ma sounds alarmed. "Child, are you all right? Did you sleep here all night?"

"Yes." I dash at my cheeks. "I'm okay, I just thought—"

"Would take more than a little fever to kill me."

"Oh my god..." I drag in a shuddering breath, "I was so afraid you would die. It was the curse—"

"What is that?" Ma is frowning at the rumpled quilt. She tugs the blanket and something heavy and shiny tumbles out. A crown.

My crown.

"Ulf's breath." Ma snatches her hand back. "How did that get here?"

I pluck it from the bed. The brilliant, red-black jewels wink at me. "Rogue must have packed it with my satchel..."

"Hello?" someone calls up the stairs. Leelah.

"We're up here!" I call. "Ma's awake."

"Thank Ulf." Leelah opens the door and stands aside as Rogue sweeps past her, bringing a platter with more mugs of tea, and plates of sweet cakes. Her jaw drops and she points at the floating tray.

"It's all right, it's just the *whisps*," I say, once again staring at the crown in my hand. "The king's wind servants I told you about yesterday."

"Right. Thank you." Leelah accepts the mug of tea Rogue brings to her, and gives a little curtsey. "I just came to tell you. The news is all over the kingdom. The curse is gone. The Red Death has passed. Everyone has recovered—the villagers are dancing in the streets."

"Are you sure?" Things are happening so fast, my head is spinning.

"It's a miracle," Leelah says.

"It is indeed." Ma straightens, reaching for a sweet cake. Something catches the light at the base of her throat.

Leelah gasps and points to Ma.

"What is it?" Ma pats her front. Her shawl has fallen open to reveal her neck and upper chest. Right there, just below her collarbone, is a huge, silver handprint—an Alpha-sized handprint. But not just any Alpha. I'd recognize the size of that paw anywhere.

"He was here," I whisper. I clutch the crown to my chest.

Rogue tugs at the blanket, revealing a small scroll. The gilded parchment unravels in front of my face and I grasp it to read:

My Rose, you forgot this. I've sent word to the Council. You are to be crowned on the morrow. The kingdom will accept your rule.

You will make a fine queen.

~ Bestian.

Beneath the signature there's a sketch of a moonflower, and the words: *Remember me.*

I shoot to my feet, my heart racing. "I have to go."

"Go?" Leelah gapes at me.

"He was here." I look about for my cloak, and Rogue whisks past me, blowing my braids on end.

"Who?" Leelah asks.

"The king," Ma says. Out of all of us, she looks the most calm. "The king was here."

"Bestian," I say. A flood of warmth spreads through my chest. Rogue returns with such force, Leelah's apron flaps into her face. It lifts my braids and fastens my cloak.

"I have to go," I tell Ma. "I must return to him."

"Of course, child." She pats my arm. "You go. I'll be fine."

"Are you sure?" I grip her hand, suddenly hesitant. "I can stay."

"You love him, don't you?"

A hundred excuses are on the tip of my tongue. *Love isn't real. It's a construct to sell greeting cards and Valentine's Day candy, and preserve the ridiculous construct of a nuclear family.* But all I say is, "Yes."

She squeezes my hand tight and releases me. "Then go. Go save him."

"How did you know—"I begin, but she interrupts me, her eyes gleaming.

"The legend tells of an Omega who saves the king, right? You're the hero of this story. Go and save your king."

***

"Go and save the king. Easier said than done," I mutter an hour later. Sweat coats my back and my knife is giving me blisters on my palm. Rogue carried me easily up

190

to the base of the castle hill but then it stopped abruptly, setting me down. "Can you get me up there?" I asked, but it ruffled my skirts sadly. So I asked it to fetch me a good knife from Ma's kitchen, and set to work.

It's slow going. The tangle of wilderness is denser than I remember, a mass of gnarly brambles and wilting moonflower blossoms. It's even harder to hack through than last time.

"Can you help me?" I ask the *whisps*. I can sense them here, at my back. All of them, not just Rogue. Bestian must have ordered them to leave the castle. To leave him.

There's a sharp ache in my heart but I'm ignoring it. I need to stay focused. Calm. Having a giant emotional breakdown on the side of this hill wouldn't help anyone.

"I need to get to him," I tell them, "and I need to do it fast. Can I..."

Wait a minute.

I extend my hand imperiously. "Make way," I order, and the vines part before me, uncovering the worn stone path. I close my eyes and expand my senses. Sure enough—I can feel it, hovering on the edges of my consciousness. The power of the land.

"Take me to him," I order, and the ground rolls beneath my feet. "Back to the castle," I order the *whisps*, and I can physically feel the chains that bound them snapping, like little electric jolts. "Make ready."

Riding the surf of lawn and wind, I arrive at the castle walls. The place looks more foreboding than before. Like a hundred years have passed. I raise a hand and the gate crashes open, disintegrating as I pass through it.

The gardens are chaotic and choked with weeds, nothing like the manicured flowerbeds of before. The *whisps* dart to and fro, blowing leaves and stalks off the paths, trimming back overgrown bushes and vines.

Looking up, I gasp with dismay. Ahead of me, the vines have grown through the windows and doors of the palace, snaking inside and, in some places, prising the stone apart. Holes gape in the roof and walls. It will take the *whisps* more than a few seconds to fix this.

"Clear a path," I order, and feed the *whisps* a little more power. A gale rushes past me, tearing into the palace, taking it apart. Piece by piece, beam by beam, the structure is dismantled. Bestian and I will create a new palace after this.

If I'm not too late.

No. I won't give up hope.

I push my shoulders back, and press on, calling his name as I enter the ruins.

I find him at the bottom of the ballroom stairs, in a bed of rotten moonflowers. My king is sprawled on his back, facing the sky. His cloak conceals most of his body, but every bare patch of his skin is a dull, mottled gray instead of vivid teal. His mask is gone, his expression still.

With my heart in my mouth, I drop to my knees beside him, seized with panic when, for a horrible moment, he doesn't seem to be breathing. I put my trembling hand on his chest and, after a few agonizing seconds, my palm rises and falls with the barest movement. My heart finally starts beating again.

"Oh Bestian, my love," I whisper. "What have you done to yourself?"

TWENTY-TWO

Bestian

AT THE FAR END OF A DARK CORRIDOR, I SCENT A HINT of something wonderful. Sweet and sharply floral—Rose's scent. There must still be some on my robe. Instead of bringing comfort, it brings the pain into sharper relief.

Unable to move my lips enough to roar, or yell, I allow myself to groan. The forlorn sound echoes in the lonely space.

"Bestian?"

Either I'm hallucinating, or I'm already dead. But then I hear it again. Louder, with a note of panic.

"Bestian?"

I struggle to focus on the blurry figure as it moves toward me. Her scent grows stronger, making me dizzy. I try to say her name but my lips won't cooperate.

"Oh Bestian, my love, what have you done to yourself?"

She's kneeling beside me, her huge brown eyes shimmering, a look of horror on her beautiful face. Ulf, I wish I could reach for her, comfort her, tell her she didn't do anything. This was my choice. My sacrifice.

And I would do it all again. For my kingdom. For her.

"Can you talk?" Her hand is on my chest but I feel nothing.

I try to speak again, and fail. I can't shake my head.

She's stroking my ravaged face with her long, elegant fingers but I can't feel her touch. Her scent is driving me out of my mind. I wish she hadn't come back. I had thought nothing could be worse than being without her, but I was wrong. Seeing and hearing my Omega in distress and not being able to do an ulfdamn thing to soothe her is infinitely worse.

Instinctually, I try to purr, but the sound is strangled in my constricted chest. I can't even do that. I'm helpless to do anything...

... except to die.

Rose

His breath whistles between his rigid lips. I can barely make out the word. "Rose."

"I'm here." I take his hand, stroking the scaly gray skin.

A groan creaks out of him.

"You did it. You saved everyone in the kingdom. You saved Ma." I press my cheek to his. His cedar scent is tainted with ash. "It's done. The curse is broken."

There's an awful rattling sound in his chest. I place my hand there, in the same place he touched Ma to heal her.

"I'm here now. Don't leave me." I bow my head, willing him to push off the effects of the curse.

This is what happened to his father. He knew it would happen. He sacrificed himself.

Remember me when the moonflowers blossom and glow.

Goosebumps shiver over my skin. When I last saw him at the beach... he was saying goodbye.

"You can't die. You haven't claimed me yet. I'm your Omega, remember? And that makes you my Alpha. We belong together!"

All around us, the *whisps* are dismantling the castle. Great chunks of the roof fly away and light streams in, gilding his features. The suns touch his marred cheeks and the disfiguring scars around his eyes. His face isn't so bad, really.

I squeeze his hand, leaning over him. My tears splash on his brow. Onto his ruined face, so beautiful to me.

"I need you," I whisper. "I want you to come back to me."

There's a pause, and I sense the whole of the castle holding its breath. The stillness rushes in and I realize... the rattling in his chest has fallen silent.

"No. No. No!" I howl. I need medicine, or magic. Something. I reach out, wildly, for anything—as if the *whisps* might have medicine or something that could help. But all that comes to hand is a moonflower vine. It will have to do.

I find a single, sharp thorn and drive it into my palm, slicing my skin. I grit my teeth against the pain and do it again, stabbing my flesh until the scarlet blood runs down my fingers.

I touch my fingertip to Bestian's lips. "Live. Live for me." I lean down close enough to kiss his cheek. "I love you."

Another second of silence. The ground quakes.

A sudden, fierce wind whips around us, blowing back my braids. Lights burst behind my eyes. The walls of the palace crumble away.

Bestian's chest is rising and falling again. I can sense

him trapped in his stone body, yearning. Connecting with my newfound magic, I reach in and pull forth his soul.

All Bestian's pain, all his wanting, and the poison saturating his body—I draw it into myself. It burns like the hottest fire and I roar, loud as an Alpha, welcoming the pain.

I am as big as the universe—and I can contain it.

There's a resounding, explosive boom, and the last of the outer walls crumble away.

Then everything goes black.

When I come to, I'm on a warm surface that's rising and falling in an easy rhythm.

With immense effort, I raise my head. I feel wrung out. "Bestian?"

The gray crust on his skin is cracking, the stony scales crumbling to dust. The scarlet rash recedes to reveal healthy, teal-colored skin with brilliant green markings. His eyes blink open and he takes a startled breath. "Rose?"

"I'm here." Tears sting my eyes. "I claimed you."

He cups my cheek. "You came for me."

"Yes," I croak. There's something flaking off my face. I touch my cheek and my finger comes away smudged with gray dust.

Bestian's eyes widen. "What is that?"

I cough. My mouth feels like it's been years since I brushed my teeth. "I think it's part of the curse."

He snaps upward, pulling me into his lap. I guess I don't have to worry about his recovery. He's patting me all over, moving all his limbs just fine. "What happened? What did you do?"

I lick my lips, tasting metal. Blood? "I did a thing. I claimed you. I think." I rub my cheek again, scraping it with my nails, feeling my face. My skin is coated in gray dust, but there's no rash, and no stony scales. I think I'm okay. But there's an ache in my chest, and when I go to rub it, Bestian does the same thing—to his own chest.

We both stare at each other.

"Can you feel that?" he asks. He places his hand on my chest, and I do the same to him. Our hearts are beating exactly in sync.

"I can feel your emotions," I say. "You're... really fucking stressed."

"Yes."

"You're alive. I guess the bond thing worked."

"You shouldn't have done it," he says, cupping my face. "Your safety, above all."

"What's the point of being queen if I don't use my magic?" I lay my palms on his cheeks. "You're healed."

"Yes. You saved me." His voice is gruff. His gorgeous green eyes are piercing my very soul.

"And you saved Medela. There's no more curse. The whole kingdom is celebrating."

"Is Ma..."

"Recovered. Completely." I mold my fingers over the rough scars of his face. "You sacrificed yourself. Thank you."

"You did it for me." He brushes more ash off my skin. "Rose, you could have died."

"You *were* dying," I counter. "But you didn't. And neither will I."

"You're so sure."

"Of course I'm sure. I'm the queen. What I say goes."

"Bossy Omega."

"Insufferable Alpha."

And we grin at each other.

Something squawks nearby—it's a brightly colored

lizard, peeking out of the foliage. A *whisp* wafts by, shooing the creature away.

"I kinda destroyed your palace. Sorry. I figured we could build a new one." I move my head to one side, stretching my neck, and something pops. More dust drifts off my skin. "But maybe we could have a nap first?"

TWENTY-THREE

My queen snuggles against me, and I rejoice in the feeling of holding her close when I never thought I would again. How could I go from the deepest, abject misery to these dizzying heights of joy in so short a time?

"Just a little sleep," she murmurs. "We have time."

"Rose." I touch her hair, her face. Breathe in her sweet scent. The side of her neck still shows evidence of the curse. A few parts are scaly and gray. But the crust is flaking off to reveal healthy, smooth skin.

She rescued me and bonded us. Somehow, her magic broke through and did the impossible. She took on part of the curse, and together, we destroyed it.

Without her, I would never have survived.

I owe her my life—a debt I can never repay. But I intend to spend the rest of my days doing all I can to make her happy. To fulfill her every desire. To rule Medela as my father wanted me to, as I should have done from the start. I am reborn. Ulf has blessed me with a second chance. And I will make the most of it

I'm still not entirely convinced this isn't just a fever dream, but I don't care if it's not real. I've never been so happy.

Rose, my mate, my Omega, is in my arms. This is where I want to be. Forever.

———

Rose

Bestian's rich scent seeps into my consciousness, waking me from my deep sleep. One huge paw slides down to cup my ass, tugging me firmly up against him, letting me feel the impressive, rigid length of his cock. He lets out a growl and my body reacts instantly with a gush of liquid desire between my thighs.

There's a gnawing, pulsing ache in my clit.

"Rose," he growls, and when I part my lips to reply, his mouth comes down on mine, stealing my words—and my breath. His kiss is long and hungry. I slide a hand up his neck, feeling his pulse thump against my palm.

He's alive. We're alive. We made it.

He breaks away and gives me a satisfied smile. Over his shoulder, the five moons have risen. Lilac moonlight streams over us. We're still in the ballroom, at the foot of the staircase. The *whisps* have cleared away all the vines and rebuilt the walls. The place feels twice as big. Rows of new onyx columns stand in rows along the sides of the room. Each one has a vine-like pattern snaking around it, gleaming a reddish purple.

Instead of a roof, the *whisps* have created an invisible barrier. Now there's nothing between us and the vast night sky.

"Wow," I breathe. "How is that even possible?"

Bestian opens his mouth and I touch a finger to his lips.

"Actually, never mind," I say. "No need to explain." Sometimes it's nice to just relax and enjoy the magic.

My mate tilts his head, catching my finger between his lips. I gasp.

"Bestian—" I begin, but then he's kissing me, his claws making short work of my clothing. His mouth never leaves mine as he slices the fabric off me. The perfumed night air whispers over my naked skin.

I'm burning up, my heart pounding in my chest. The ache between my thighs is exquisite.

Bestian growls, sending vibrations singing through my entire body. He tastes like bonfire smoke and marshmallows. If he doesn't get inside me soon, I'll die. I'm sure of it.

He lifts me into his lap and I go willingly. He rains kisses over me... across my jawline, along my neck, over the slope of my breast. Taking a taut nipple between his sharp teeth, he nips it, and the sharp zing of pain makes me gasp. I don't know whether I'm relieved or disappointed when he forgoes my other nipple and continues on his way down... kissing my ribs, my belly, my hip bone.

His claw shreds the last of my clothing—silky Ulfarri bloomers. He tears the delicate fabric off me, tossing it aside.

The *whisps* created a soft bed of blankets and pillows beneath us at the base of the stairs. Bestian rears up and yanks off his cloak. He looms over me, and for a moment, my breath catches. He's a massive, scary beast, imposing in the moonlight.

But then the bond between us flares to life, and I sense his lust. His love.

"Bestian." I reach for him but he stops me with a command.

"Lie still."

He's in bossy mode. It's on. We're doing this.

I stretch out before him, letting him look his fill at my naked form. He rumbles his approval and braces himself over me.

"Beautiful," he breathes. He moves down my body, nuzzling my breasts and stomach until my perfume bursts from my pores. The floral scent melds with his heady musk.

I part my legs without being asked, desperate for his tongue to find the place where I need it the most, but he teases me mercilessly, licking and nibbling down the inside of one thigh, then up the other side.

"Please," I croak, my voice thick with lust. "Please."

"Shhh," he whispers, his fingertips closing around my nipples and pinching them savagely. My pussy flutters.

Falling silent, I wait, praying to a god I don't believe in that he won't torture me too much longer. After an interminable amount of time, he grips my ankles in his huge hands and spreads my legs wide to the point of pain before bending his head and licking me from pussy to clit in one broad, slow sweep.

I'm so splayed open that my labia is already parted for him and he takes advantage of this, repeating that lick again... and then again...

It feels so good, but it's too slow. I need more on my clit. I start writhing in his grip, trying to move my hips to get his tongue where I want it.

"Naughty Omega," he growls, "don't move. Lie still and just let this happen."

"But—" I protest even as his words send my desire ratcheting higher.

"If you keep wriggling, I'll stop," he says.

Surely he wouldn't... would he? Then his tongue finds my clit again and I cry out at the pleasure of it.

I'm naked, vulnerable, helpless to do anything but lie

here with this huge beast holding my legs apart and licking me with impossibly slow, deliberate, agonizing precision.

I'm so close to coming that my legs are trembling, but every time I'm about to fall over the edge he changes it up, licks around the place where I need him to, or fucks me with his tongue until I'm almost incoherent.

"Fuck... please!" I howl, too far gone to care that I'm begging. He lets go of my ankles, and rears up. "No, wait!" He can't stop licking me now. He just can't! I haven't come yet!

"So bossy. So beautiful." His gorgeous eyes glow as he tears off the rest of his clothes and reaches for me, flipping me over until I'm lying on my belly, then tugging my thighs apart once more.

I feel the huge, blunt head of his cock being lined up with my sopping hole and gasp, suddenly afraid. He's never done this without giving me at least one orgasm to loosen me up. What if I can't take him?

"Lift your hips a little," he whispers and I find myself obeying automatically, the way I always respond to his commands. Like he's cast some kind of spell over me.

His hand snakes around my hip and finds my slick pussy, spreading my labia with his index and ring fingers and caressing my swollen, pulsing clit with his middle finger. Instantly, I'm back on the brink of orgasm but then he decreases the pressure, edging me with light, barely there strokes.

"Take it all," he growls in my ear, rolling his hips until the head of his cock is directly between my folds, "there's my good girl. You're so tight... so slick... so beautiful."

There's a searing ache in my sex as he enters me, forcing me to stretch impossibly wide around him.

"You can do it," he coaxes, "just a little more, a little

deeper... when I'm all the way in, I'll give you the release you so desperately need."

Once again, I'm taken aback by the sheer size of him as he enters me. It hurts—maybe just because he's big, maybe because I haven't had an orgasm yet—but the pain is a perfect counterpoint to the tingles of pleasure his fingertip is inducing in my clit.

I'm lying naked, face down on the pillows with my ass in the air, my knees spread wider than they have any right to be. He's pinning me down with his other hand on the back of my neck, and I can't escape. I have no choice but to lie here and take it.

Take his impossibly big cock, and the even bigger knot that will follow.

Take the pain he's dishing out.

And take the orgasm he's promised me, the one he's been cruelly denying me this entire time.

As if he heard my thoughts, Bestian bottoms out inside me with a grunt of pleasure. "My perfect little moonflower, being such a good girl," he whispers. "Are you ready to come for me? I want to feel that tight, slick cunt clenching around my cock..." As he speaks, he increases the pressure on my clit just enough, and that combination sends me hurtling over the edge.

I've never felt anything like it. Inhuman, guttural noises are coming out of me as my clit jerks beneath his relentless fingertip, each spasm of ecstasy starting right there and rolling through my entire body. My pussy is rippling uncontrollably, trying but failing to contract around his rigid girth.

"Yes," he's still coaxing me, "just like that... keep coming for me, sweetheart. Relax and just let it happen, don't stop, don't fight it... Your hot, wet little cunt feels so good clenching around me like that, milking me, I don't want it to stop until I spill my seed..."

I can't take it anymore, it's too much, it feels too good... there's no way I can keep coming until he comes. And yet I haven't crested the peak yet, I'm still riding that wave, my entire body rigid beneath him, shuddering, a part of me dimly wondering how in the fuck he can make an orgasm last this long.

"No, please," I whimper, but my words are muffled by the cushions.

"Almost there, little one," he croons, his fingertip still moving over my aching, hyper-sensitive clit. "Feel the knot?"

The searing burn of his knot forming, stretching me wider, only serves to increase my pleasure. "Yes," I moan.

"I'm ready." His voice is husky, seductive. He's so in control, while I'm beside myself with the force of this endless orgasm. "I love how responsive you are. How you keep coming when I tell you to, like a good little girl. How you let me use you to milk my cock, your tight, slick pussy squeezing me so hard as you come that I can barely stand how good it feels."

His words are so naughty and humiliating, my face is on fire even as my pleasure goes up yet another notch.

His hand leaves the back of my neck. He's leaning down, covering me, his breath hot in my ear. "Almost there, my moonflower, you're almost ready..."

I'm about to ask him what for when a searing, exquisite pain shoots through the place where my neck meets my shoulder. The pleasure is so intense, my endless orgasm peaks at last and I howl into the pillow, my hopelessly stretched pussy contracting over and over again. With his teeth still embedded in my flesh, Bestian comes with a muffled roar, his cock jerking violently inside me as he floods me with his cum.

When at last he's spent, he slumps down over me, his huge body heavy against mine. I welcome the touch of his skin. His warmth covering me. I feel light-headed, drowsy, and absurdly happy.

We lie that way for an eternity, joined together in two places, two hearts beating as one, waiting for our breathing to slow.

A sharp sting tugs me out of my contented doze—Bestian's teeth leaving my neck. Then there's a wet, tingling sensation in the same place. He's licking the wound.

For a second, I wonder whether that's hygienic but then I figure: fuck it. He's a nerd about these things. No doubt he knows what he's doing. So I close my eyes and let the pleasant feelings wash over me.

When he finally speaks, his voice is tender. "It's done, my sweet Rose. I've claimed you as mine. We were already bonded, but now we're soul-bonded. Joined together... forever."

"I love you," I mumble into the pillow. "I think you already know that but I wanted to say it." *Now that you're alive again. Now that you can hear me.*

"Oh, my sweet little moonflower," Bestian whispers, his breath on my neck making me shiver, "I love you too. And I always will. My Omega. My queen."

EPILOGUE

O~NE YEAR LATER...~

Rose

For the first time in forever, laughter fills the palace. The entire ballroom is glowing, not from the orbs, but from strategically placed bouquets of moonflowers. Every time a guest enters, they blink and point with awe.

Ma glides up to me, arm-in-arm with Leelah, who looks nervous.

"Are you having fun?" I ask.

"Of course," Ma says. She looks radiant in her silvery-pink gown. She even let Rogue do her hair.

"I can't believe I'm in the same room as *four kings*," Leelah whispers, her eyes wide.

"I know, right?" I say and wave at Bestian across the room. He gives me a dazzling smile and my heart skips a beat. We kicked the midnight ball off with a formal receiving line, but between the welcome and the first dance, we decided we'd mingle.

Bestian is standing with a group of kings—Khan the

Wanderer King, Aurus the Golden King, and the Hunter King. We sent invitations to all the known kings, but received no reply from three: the Demon King, the King of Ruins, and the King of the Wastes. Bestian assured me he had expected as much.

Too bad. I was looking forward to seeing what they all looked like, but especially the Demon King. One scroll I found described him as a monster, with giant horns and purple skin. But that's probably an exaggeration.

Then again, anything is possible. Even magic.

Ma wrinkles her nose at the assembled rulers. She's not impressed by royalty. She's the kind of person who feels at home anywhere, especially a palace.

Ma didn't want to abandon her cottage to come and live with us, but she visits us so often, she has her own set of rooms. She loves the gardens, but our favorite place to spend time together is the Queen's study, where she and I spend hours poring over ancient scrolls.

Together, we've founded the Royal Academy of Omegas. So far, our focus has been on studying herbs and remedies for pregnant and nursing Omegas. The human-Omega queens visit us regularly for checkups. Kim is seven months pregnant with what she calls *Aurus's spawn*, and as is apparent by the slight bump under her exquisite lilac dress, Emma is working on baby number two.

"I meant to tell you," I say to Ma. "Haley asked if she could see us tomorrow. For a checkup."

"Oh!" Ma's eyes light up. "Which one is Haley?"

I point to the three human queens who have commandeered a set of chaises in the corner. "She's the brown-haired one in the green gown. The Hunter King's mate." No one knows the Hunter King's real name. I asked Haley what we should call him, and she said he prefers to just go by *Hunter*.

I like the Hunter King. He's very quiet—I don't think I've ever heard him say more than three words in the entire time I've known him—but he looks at Haley like she's his world. And his silence is a welcome contrast to Aurus's non-stop arrogant posturing. I don't know how Kim puts up with the Golden King but then, she's pretty loud, too. She can certainly hold her own with him. They seem like a perfect match—in fact, that could be said for all three royal couples. The more I learn about it, the more I get the impression this Alpha-Omega mating thing has a clear advantage over relationships back home.

"Rose!" Kim shouts across the ballroom. She's on a sturdy chaise with her feet up and a plate of sweet cakes balanced on her big, pregnant belly.

"Excuse me," I murmur to Ma and Leelah, and head to my fellow queens with Rogue hot on my heels. The little *whisp* outdid itself on my hair and gown, and has followed me around all night to hold up both my bejeweled hairstyle and my train, so both float effortlessly in the air.

Emma and Haley smile at me from their seats on the chaise.

I've almost reached Kim's side when the plate of sweet cakes goes flying.

"Holy shit, did you see that?" Kim cries. "The baby just kicked the plate right off me!"

We assure her we saw it.

"Damn, this kid is going to be a handful," she says cheerfully. "I already told Aurus he's on diaper duty."

"Good," I say, eyeing her belly. "Because there's a real chance that baby is going to be bigger than you within a few weeks."

Kim snickers and so does Emma, but Haley palms her own stomach, looking alarmed.

"I'm kidding," I tell her.

"Oh, of course," she says, dropping her hand. But she's
been touching her belly all night long. Supposedly she's
coming to the appointment tomorrow for a basic checkup,
but I wouldn't be surprised if we get a positive pregnancy
test.

"You look beautiful," Emma says, her blue eyes wide as
she takes in my shimmering red-purple gown.

"Thanks. So do you."

"How do you get your hair to float like that?" Kim asks.

"Magic," I murmur. Rogue ruffles the curls at the base
of my neck.

A light trilling sound, much like the song of the singing
lizards, signals the start of the music. It's time for the first
dance. The flute-like sound swells into a majestic march,
played by the royal musicians at the end of the ballroom.

A prickle runs up my spine, followed by a swelling
sense of contentment. I don't have to turn my head to know
that Bestian is behind me.

He places a large hand on my back, and I savor his
delicious scent. "Pardon me, Your Majesties," he says. "As
the hosts, I believe the first dance is ours."

I grin at my friends and let Bestian guide me away to
the center of the room. He twirls me out across the
dancefloor and we acknowledge our guests with a bow and
curtsey in a choreographed movement that would make the
pomp-and-circumstance lovers proud. I rise and face him,
and the heat in his eyes takes my breath away.

He's not wearing a mask. I know he has one that
matches my gown. I even suggested we make this ball a
masquerade. Masks are *en vogue* now, ever since Bestian
first ventured out of the palace wearing his. All the high-
fashion people in Medea City wear them to mimic the king.

When he demurred against a masquerade, I didn't
realize he meant he'd also leave his mask off. He doesn't

wear one around me, but it makes him more comfortable around other people.

I take his outstretched hand and squeeze it. "You look gorgeous," I say.

"That's what I was going to say."

We share a smile.

All around us, our guests are watching, but it's easy to forget them and pretend it's just the two of us here.

He pulls me into his arms and we begin to dance. He leads me in the steps—an elegant blend of traditional Medii dance steps and a formal Earth-style waltz.

He tugs me closer, and the wind surges under my feet.

Below us, the crowd gasps. We're floating on an invisible platform, right up to the sky.

And then we're alone, because we've risen right up through the magical ceiling and out across the garden. I laugh.

"What amuses you?" he asks.

"You amuse me. We invited a bunch of guests over, organized a fancy-ass ball, and now we're dancing all alone outside."

"King's prerogative." He looks smug. But through the bond, I can sense his other emotions—his pride and power, his desire to protect me, his adoration.

His love.

"I guess it's okay for a little while," I say. "But then we have to go back. We do have responsibilities, as hosts."

"Bossy Omega."

"You love it."

"I do. Ulf help me. I do." And with that, he spins me around to the music of our laughter, dancing in the air over endless fields of glowing moonflowers.

Just like in a fairytale.

THE END

Want more delicious growly Alpha-hole knottiness?
CLICK HERE TO PREORDER THE DEMON KING'S STORY NOW!

Planet of Kings
Brutal Mate - Book 1
Brutal Claim - Book 2
A gift for the Alpha - freebie when you sign up to our newsletter
Brutal Capture - Book 3
Brutal Beast - Book 4
Brutal Demon - Book 5

ABOUT LEE SAVINO

Lee Savino is a USA today bestselling author of smexy romance. Smexy, as in "smart and sexy." Find her in the Goddess Group on facebook and download a free book at www.leesavino.com!

Find her at:
www.leesavino.com

Want more growly alphas? Check out the Berserker Saga. Start with Sold to the Berserkers.

Remember to download your free book at www. leesavino.com

The Berserker Saga

Sold to the Berserkers – Brenna, Samuel & Daegan
Mated to the Berserkers - – Brenna, Samuel & Daegan
Bred by the Berserkers (FREE novella only available at www.leesavino.com) - – Brenna, Samuel & Daegan
Taken by the Berserkers – Sabine, Ragnvald & Maddox
Given to the Berserkers – Muriel and her mates
Claimed by the Berserkers – Fleur and her mates

Ménage Sci Fi Romance

Draekons (Dragons in Exile) with Lili Zander (ménage
alien dragons)

*Crashed spaceship. Prison planet. Two big, hulking, bronzed
aliens who turn into dragons. The best part? The dragons
insist I'm their mate.*

Paranormal romance

Bad Boy Alphas with Renee Rose (bad boy werewolves)
Never ever date a werewolf.

Possessive Warrior Sci fi romance

Draekon Rebel Force with Lili Zander
Start with Draekon Warrior

Tsenturion Warriors with Golden Angel
Start with Alien Captive

Contemporary Romance

Royal Bad Boy
*I'm not falling in love with my arrogant, annoying, sex god
boss. Nope. No way.*

Royally Fake Fiancé
*The Duke of New Arcadia has an image problem only a
fiancé can fix. And I'm the lucky lady he's chosen to play
Cinderella.*

Beauty & The Lumberjacks
After this logging season, I'm giving up sex. For...reasons.

Her Marine Daddy
My hot Marine hero wants me to call him Daddy...

Her Dueling Daddies
Two daddies are better than one.

Innocence: dark mafia romance with Stasia Black
I'm the king of the criminal underworld. I always get what I want. And she is my obsession.

Beauty's Beast: a dark romance with Stasia Black
Years ago, Daphne's father stole from me. Now it's time for her to pay her family's debt...with her body.

ABOUT TABITHA BLACK

I love to write steamy romance where the men are deviant, dominant, and delicious, and the heroines simply can't resist them - and really, who can blame them?

I've lived all over the world but am currently in the UK, where the people are lovely but the weather... not so much!

My current project is a seriously hot, dark, sci-fi romance series called Savages in the Shadows. The prequel is free, and you can get your copy here: Rescued Mate

I just adore getting mail, so if you want to drop me a line, please do so at tabitha_black@hotmail.com. Please also feel free to sign up for my newsletter, follow me on BookBub, or join my Shameless Readers on Facebook. Thank you for reading!

Don't miss these other exciting books by Tabitha Black!

Paranormal

Planet of Kings - With Lee Savino
Brutal Mate - Book 1
Brutal Claim - Book 2
Brutal Capture - Book 2
Brutal Beast - Book 4
Brutal Demon - Book 5 (Preorder now!)

Alphas of Sandor
Primal Possession - Book 1

Primal Mate - Book 2

Contemporary BDSM

His Empire Series
Restraint - Book 1
Denial - Book 2
Anticipation - Novella

Masters of the Castle Series
Fulfilling Her Fantasy
Sharing Silver
Tempting Tasha
Undoing Una

Midnight Doms
Her Vampire Addiction

Anthologies
When the Gavel Falls (Sharing Silver)
Witness Protection Program (Tempting Tasha)
Dominating His Valentine (Anticipation)
Daddies of the Castle (Undoing Una)

Audiobooks
Little Tudor Rose
Conquering Cassia
Restraint
Sapphire's Surrender
Primal Possession

www.ingramcontent.com/pod-product-compliance
Lightning Source LLC
Chambersburg PA
CBHW061120100726

47911CB00013B/622